BigFoot moon:
formerly The American Quarterly Review

a novel

A. B. Paulson

TRIGLYPH BOOKS
PORTLAND OREGON

TriGlyph Books
6312 SW Capitol Hwy
Suite 242
Portland, Oregon 97239

Photo Credits

Photo (p. 38) used by permission of The Maryhill Museum of Art. Photos (pp. 119 & 170) used by permission of The City of Portland Archives. All other photos are from Bigstock.com, the Library of Congress, or by the author.

Manufactured in the United States of America

Library of Congress Control Number: 2017913963

ISBN 978-0-692-94631-2

Acknowledgments

Special thanks to Tom Buell, Glen Gillespie, Marjorie Burns, Paul Giles, Holly Marcus, Colleen Wilks, Barbara Guetti, and the family of the late Wayne Jensen. Thanks to Linda Morrell for the keyboard of the Chopin Prelude. For encouragement over the years, thanks to Gary Goss, Peter Carafiol, John Smythe, Tracy Dillon, and to my family: Trilby, Chris, and Jayden.

A Note on the Text

This hardcopy form of *BigFoot Moon* mirrors the page numbering of the MAC DIGITAL/INTERACTIVE version (see *BigFootMoon.com*). <u>Underlined</u> words and phrases in this print version indicate interactive items on the digital. Sorry, no color, sound or videos in this version.

The Sasquatch Alphabet and typeface was adapted from the Shaw Alphabet as published in Bernard Shaw's *Androcles and the Lion,* The Shaw Alphabet Edition, (Penguin Books Ltd: Harmonsworth, Middlesex, 1962).

In 1958, not far from Ferlinghetti's City Lights Bookstore, Bill Caxton produced a mimeographed booklet ambitiously titled *The American Quarterly Review*. As it's evolved and grown over time, the magazine has reflected the changing landscape of American literary culture. Now a young editorial staff offers you a glimpse of its most recent incarnation: digital AQR.

(Here formatted for print.)

In this Issue

Coming West
a View from the Pacific-End of America
Fiction—Essays—Artifacts
Guest Editor: Art Strether

A Word from the Editor

Hello—
I'm Bill Caxton.
I'm taking a break for
the next two
issues. In my place,
Wynk de Worde will
be taking over.

VOLUME XLIII NO. 3   FALL 2001

THE AMERICAN QUARTERLY REVIEW

*A Journal of Fiction, Poetry, Literary History,
and Cultural Criticism*

FOUNDING EDITOR
Bill Caxton

ACTING EDITOR
Wynk de Worde

GUEST EDITOR
Art Strether

BUSINESS MANAGER
Gordon Sable

EDITORIAL ASSISTANT
Edward Gayles

FILM CONSULTANTS
Paul Newman &
 Joanne Woodward

EDITORIAL ADVISORY BOARD
Wayne C. Booth, *Univ. of Chicago*
Jacques Derrida, *Ecole des Hautes
Etudes en Sciences Sociales*
Leslie Fiedler, *SUNY Buffalo*
Norman Holland, *Univ. FL Gainesville*
J. Hillis Miller, *Univ. CA Irvine*
John Price, *Dartmouth College*

DESIGNERS
Wynk de Worde
AND Madeline Goedieff

The American Quarterly Review is published quarterly by AQR Publications, Inc. a not-for-profit corporation, 408 Melrose, Vanport, Cascadia. Contributions to AQR Publications, Inc. are tax deductible to the extent permitted by law; make checks payable to W. de Worde. Editorial and business correspondence should be addressed to the above address. Advertising inquiries, or letters of a personal nature, should be directed to Wynk de Worde at 776 Atrium Place, Vanport, Cascadia. Manuscripts, to be returned, must be accompanied by a self-addressed 9x12 envelope with sufficient first-class return postage—no clever or commemorative stamps, please. The editors can assume no responsibility for loss, damage, or mutilation of any work submitted. All details, especially citations, should conform to the *1977 MLA Style Manual.* Manuscripts accepted for publication become the property of AQR Publications, Inc., and the editors assume some latitude in making editorial adjustments. No essays, poetry, or fiction accepted from June to October, Dec. 15-31, March 1-15, January 19 through February 17, April 1st, April 20 to May 19. No multiple submissions. No breezy cover letters. Do not telephone to inquire about whether we received your manuscript. Please allow 18 to 24 months for a response.

we find things— anywhere.

Zapf Private Detective Agency
Pioneer Square, PDX, OR

In our Next Issue:
"Our Greatest American Detective Novelist"

Ross McDonald (1915 - 1983)

Our Lovely **Yak Hat** is hand-knit from rare Mongolian & Finnish fibers.
S-M-L $79.95 +S&H

Box 487
Goose Hollow OR

Just Frogs

Costume fasteners, floral bases, rail switches, live specimens for dissection: 27 shades of green. Free Catalog: Box 2 Boring, OR.

Fatima / Twin Cities Press
Congratulates Garland Lovejoy
on winning the *Hubert Humphrey Award*
for the Allusive Sestina.

Contents

Daddy?
An investigative report by Zolar Zapf 33
Abstract. Certain irregularities in Plath's birth
certificate lead to the Stonehenge of the Northwest

Hemingway, Gertrude Stein and
    the Art of the Sestina

Abstract. A newly discovered manuscript for
The Song of Hiawatha indicates Longfellow's
debt to an pre-Columbian alphabet.

LETTERS

A PARDONER EXCHANGE

To the Editors:

I must take exception to Alfreda Clapp's overly ingenious reading ["'Shryned in an Hogges Toord': Filthy Lucre and Self-(Re)flexion in The Pardoner's Tale," AQR, Spring 2001] of Harry Bailly's "literal" threat to castrate the Pardoner and cast his testicles, as she says, "like pearls, before swine."

For one thing, it is the Pardoner who invokes the exchange of scatological metaphors when he says, "kisse my relics" (for this reading see Ellesmere and Cambridge Gg) with its excremental pun on L. reliquiae—cf. Sanskrit *rinakti*: what is left behind and abandoned. Hence, Bailly's not-very-imaginative reference to the fellow's pants, as one might gloss it, being "full of shit."

More significant, as any undergraduate recalls from the "General Prologue," Chaucer's con-man lacks certain distinguishing marks of masculinity: "A voys he hadde as smal as hath a goot. / No berd hadde he, ne nevere sholde have; / As smothe it was as it were late shave. / I trowe he were a geldyng or a mare." In other words, the host's threat is an empty bluff; why threaten to castrate a eunuch?

G. Auriol, Professor of Middle English
State Univ. of N.Y. at Ithaca

To the Editors:

Prof. Clapp's discussion of Chaucer's Pardoner shook loose in my mind a curious memory. As a young man, studying in London after the War, I was shown—by a Hampstead antiquarian—a small cedar box with brass claps and hinges. Inside was a kind of soft leather bag, pleated to resemble a scrotal sac. 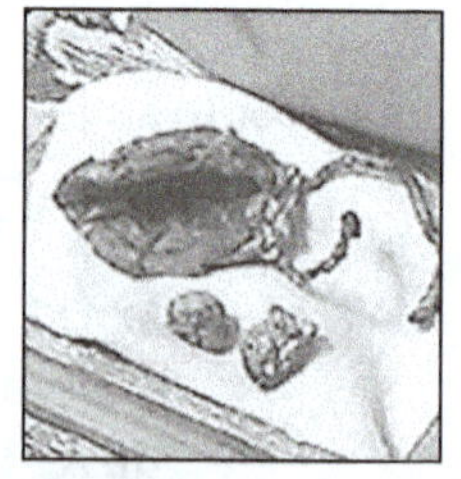

From within fell out two dry and crusty objects, about

["Letters" continued on p. 17]

The Editor's Column

Art Strether

Imagine choosing the character you'd play in the story of your life. Then wonder how I got chosen to sit in the editor's chair of Bill Caxton's magazine. *The American Quarterly Review* has a long history, and back in the Midwest, we've read and admired it since the 1960s. But now, in 2001, we know that small literary presses are struggling. That makes my job, for an issue or two, more challenging.

When I flew out here two months ago, his wife met me at the Portland airport. Margo Caxton is a trim, striking woman—perhaps in her early fifties.[1] That day she wore khaki slacks, a blouse of electric blue open at the throat, and insisted on carrying one of our bags out to the car, an old Beetle Volkswagen. It was a brilliant summer day, one of those afternoons in the Northwest when the transparency of

---

[1] Margo's youthful looks seems to change with the ambience of light—some say with the density of sound in certain rooms when the treble and bass are adjusted randomly

the atmosphere—washed clean in a long transit across the Pacific—gives glimpses of distant, but glittering, possibilities.

"Well," smiled Margo, settling in behind the wheel. "You're to be our house-guest. B.C. insists." The depth of her gray eyes—they're rumored to have inspired certain passionate lines in the poetry of Richard Wilbur, Mark Strand, and Ted Hughes—made us a little breathless.

On the Interstate, we clutched the upholstery as she deftly wove the little VW in and out of traffic. On a straight-away, we glanced at the speedometer: 110 miles per hour.

"It's got a Porsche engine!" she shouted above the noise. "I bought it used from our old neighbor, Paul Newman. That was back in Connecticut— after his son died."

An exit-sign whizzed past. "Hold on!" she

How fast can Margo's Volkswagen accelerate from a standing start? She says, "Zero to sixty in 6 seconds."

cried, took the turn, and braked hard going down the exit ramp. When we opened our eyes, we'd halted at a stop sign. Abruptly she swung a hard right, shot us through a tree-covered lane, and spun the vehicle through a series of skidding turns that threw up a plume of gravel.

Back at the main highway, she checked the rear-view mirror. "I think we lost him."

"You're joking," we said.

"Sometimes I'm followed," she laughed. "Always from the airport."

And we laughed, too—feeling hip—as if we'd been admitted to a zone of unspoken understandings, a tangled landscape of irony whose airy heights above the tree-line dropped abruptly into dark gorges and white water. Transported to such a place, what choice do you have except to trust your guide and put your life—<u>such as it is</u>—into her hands?

The Caxton house sits on a forested ridge with views to the east of Mount St. Helens and Mt. Hood. In the guest wing, Margo showed us down a corridor. Our room, at the far end, had a big bay window flanked by high bookshelves. We looked out at a stand of Douglas fir, aware that she was watching us.

"In this light" we heard her say, "you look like a fine young man." She stood leaning in the doorway, an arm clasped under her breasts, the fingertips of one hand touching her mouth.

"I'm not that young," we said. "But the view here is wonderful. And this nice room— It's really for me?"

She nodded, then looked serious. "Bill genuinely needs your help," she said. "With the magazine, I mean. He's a bit—preoccupied."

I stood still, aware of her scent, imagining moments when we'd be alone together.

Finally she took a breath and let it out. "You might as well know," she said. "Everyone else knows! Bill got some girl pregnant—years ago. In the 50s, he was a beatnik with a sailboat. He waded ashore in Oregon and fell in love—" She sighed. "Lately a private <u>detective</u> has been making some inquiries. Isn't that interesting?"

"Everyone knows this?"

"Oh Bill made a big announcement to the staff. And sent some notices to newspapers around the country: <u>Lost Son Sought</u>. That sort of thing. A couple impostors showed up. That's when they hired a detective."

"They?"

"Gordon and Bill. Gordon Sable has been Bill's business manager for years. He went to law school and knows about things like detectives. Meanwhile, manuscripts and correspondence have been piling up."

"Well," we said. "It all sounds very distracting—from your husband's editorial work, I mean."

"Yes." She was looking at a watercolor, framed, on the wall: *The Cove North of Manzanita.* "Of course, we never had children," she said.

"I see."

"Isn't it silly, how men get a little nuts about having—a <u>Jⁿdıℓ</u>* heir?"

"I suppose."

"Goodness, I'm boring you," she said, walking to the door. "I want to show you off to B.C. And the staff. They've convened—" She made a face. "—one of their *meetings.* Why don't you freshen up? Then come out to the deck."

"Fine."

"Oh, the bathroom's the next door down. Most days you'll want to take your shower early—the staff will be in and out of their cubicals all morning."

---

*Caxton shudders at profanity.

From somewhere now came the sound of vaguely festive music.

"And if you run into a short-haired distraught woman taking blue pills," said Margo, "that's Maddy. She thinks she's been fired. Okay?"

"I think I can remember all that," we said—to her back. Margo had walked out of sight.

We unpacked a few things, then checked out the bathroom. There were lots of fresh towels. The next room had a dark shade on the window—evidently a place to take naps. There was a cot and something huddled under a blanket.

It was a woman! She sat up. "Gordy?" she said, glancing at us through bleary eyes. Then she flopped down and went back to sleep. She was lovely, in a faded way. But her hair was long, and she didn't look distraught. She may have been wearing a nightgown. "Sorry," we whispered and backed out. Damn this chastity vow.

At the end of the hallway was a door with a window in it. Evidently a long corridor led somewhere—probably to the cubicals Margo had mentioned. We dared to click it open. Outside, we found our way to a flagstone path that wound through rhododendrons and stepped down in stages to a cedar deck. Past a yellow Lab sleeping on its paws, a dozen people had pulled chairs into a semi-circle. They held drinks and sat facing Caxton, who sprawled in a canvas director's chair. His tan face, the gray mustache, and white hair swept back from a high forehead recalled photos of the late Erik Erikson. A low wrought-iron table was cluttered with file folders, an ashtray, and a half-empty bottle of Early Times.

"Look what I found at the airport," said Margo.

Caxton looked up from his work. Then he muttered to the woman next to him, "𐑰𐑤 𐑒𐑭𐑛𐑕 𐑒𐑩𐑛 𐑜𐑳 𐑢𐑦𐑤𐑟 𐑕 𐑪𐑤𐑰 𐑘𐑛..." It was not an unfamiliar remark.

Over Thirty Years' Experience
Small Class Sizes Nice Tents
   Museums   Campfires
Theater   **Shaw Phonetic**
Shopping   **Alphabet**
Bring this ad for a discount.
On the Heath, London N.W. 3.

Suddenly gunshots sounded from inside the house! A woman screamed. *[continued on page 52]*

Before proceeding to page 52. please take—and *pass—* **Quiz #1** on p. 232

[continued from p. 10]
the size of acorns. The shop owner assured me that I was holding the mummified testicles of one Gwion Llanfair, a Pardoner licensed in Aberystwyth about the year 1400.

I fumbled the things back into the bag and edged toward the exit, certain I was in the presence of a madman. But I was forced to listen as the gentleman explained their history: that they'd been in the custody of a monastery near Avignon until the 19th-century; that their ritual display was said to have cured palsy and sweetened the voice of choir boys; etc. In the 1920s, Pound is reported to have seen them in Rapallo. After disappearing in Dresden during the War, they apparently made their way back to England in private hands.

Is it possible that Chaucer's seemingly playful reference to a castrated Pardoner was based upon an actual event?

William Dwiggins, Santa Barbara, California

Alfreda Clapp replies:

About the reality of what Mr. Dwiggins may have observed—still less held in his hand—some fifty years ago, I have no comment.

But I am happy to air in public a little of the discussion that Prof. Auriol and I have carried on in private for many years. Dense as usual, Auriol misses my point. The host's aggressive display retreats from metaphor in the same sense that an analyst's interpretation probes the literal-mindedness of infantile fantasy. We find no lack of potency—that is, phallic manipulative power—in the Pardoner's performance. In a word, he's got balls. But his genital impulses operate from within a shell of anal defenses. In this way, he is at once pilgrim and the very relic ("enshrined within a hog's turd") to which he pays homage. Of course, Bailly's insight—like Prof. Auriol's—is fired off from the dirty trench of squeamish self-righteousness. Given an adolescent devotion to signs construed as commodities, we understand why the ostensibly filthy spectacle of self-reference so intimidates a conventional critic.

—September 5, 2001

BARTHELME A FAKE?

To the Editors:

The Winter 2000 number of *The American Quarterly Review* contains a story called "Mahler's Massapequa" and signed with my name. As it happens, I did not write it. It is quite a worthy effort, as pastiches go, and particularly successful in reproducing my weaknesses. May I say, for whatever it's worth, that only manuscripts offered to editors by my agent, Lynn Nesbit, are authentic—not good or bad, but at least authentic.

Donald Barthelme
113 W 11 St. New York City

Mr. Barthelme, author of *The Dead Father*, is—sadly, but of course—deceased. Accordingly, he could not have written this preposterous letter. As a matter of policy, we don't print forged documents—though you would be surprised at some of the howlers that arrive at our editorial offices. This case, however, provides an occasion to reiterate how scrupulously we

Donald
Barthelme

acquired the rights to "Posthumous Works" for the Spring issue. And belated but grateful acknowledgement is made to Robert E. Smith, Director of Archives, University of Houston Library, for long hours sorting through dusty files in the stacks and for permitting us to print previously unpublished fiction by Barthelme, Robert Penn Warren, and Lillian Hellman.

CURMUDGEONS

To the Editors:

Please cancel my subscription to *AQR*. The intrusion of commercial advertising into your pages both saddens and disgusts me. The entire look and feel of the publication has recently taken a wrong turn. Bring back my old magazine.

H. Hoffman
South Bend, Indiana

The *Review* has recently made several reciprocal agreements with other quarterlies and literary presses for tasteful announcements of recent publications. We regret offending Mr. Hoffman. But we're delighted to add Wynk de Worde's name to our masthead. He and an assistant have quietly been giving some of our pages a new look.

To the Editors:

I was glad to learn—in Frederic Warde's discussion, "Spectacle: The Lowest Element in Tragedy"—that Marxist and postmodern theorists of media, have re-examined *opsis* in the *Poetics*. But wasn't Aristotle's original point simply that a reader with a text could experience pity and fear without seeing the *sounds* and *colors* of the stage production?

Lucian Bernhard,
Department of English
Washington State University at Roslyn

We observe that in Aristotle's lost treatise on *Comedy*, Spectacle ranks higher.

To the Associate Editor:

In regard to your recent inquiry, we have no Robert E. Smith on our library's staff. The University's Personnel Department tells me that a "Bob Smith" was employed by the University last year as a custodian. If you have further questions, I suggest you direct your correspondence to the Department of Buildings and Grounds.

Stanley Morison
Director of Libraries
University of Houston

THE MAGAZINE'S NEW FORMAT
To the Editor:

I've heard the rumors and made some inquiries. Is it true we'll soon have a *wireless* edition of *AQR* that fits in the palm of one's hand?

Your younger readers will be especially delighted to navigate your magazine with a few taps of a finger. Good riddance to the tedious nuisance of turning pages!

Gary Goss
Graduate Student.
State Univ. of N.Y. at Buffalo

Caxton Makes a Rare Personal Reply

Dear Mr. Goss:

Your upbeat hopes for a wireless, hand-held edition of this paper-and-ink magazine brought to mind an ardent young fellow my staff brought in last year—a skinny kid with thick glasses who held out a black gadget

He claimed the device was The future of print media, and he invited me to load some text into it as a demonstration.

Well— I wish you could experience the disheartening tedium of the thing. Who could endure more than 30 seconds of fuzzy print, drifting upwards like noxious fumes?

So, for the next six months of the year 2000, I was dead set against any digital tampering with my magazine. Then this fellow de Worde appeared and convinced me that he could preserve the old feel of turning pages on screen. So look for a change.

Now about your itch to "point-and-click." I've observed people—oh, at airports and in the waiting room at the dentist—thumbing through magazines. Some actually start at the end and flip pages backwards! Don't they realize the time and effort we spend composing the pages from the beginning?

> My ideal reader would be Faulkner's character, Joe Christmas.

My ideal reader would be Faulkner's character, Joe Christmas. Perhaps you recall that he read his magazine "straight through as though it were a novel."

I've told Wynk that I don't want my readers jumping around on screen as if they were beaming up to other levels instead of turning pages. He said he can fix that—mostly.

Fiction

The Calling

by
Frank Goudy

When the phone rang at 3 a.m., Strether went a little limp. His first question was: now who's died? One of his parents? His aging father fallen in the bathroom? The big man finally brought down by some internal thing, a bowel obstruction, a burst vessel? The toilet bowl full of blood. Horrible. Or Maybe Hester had smashed up the car—rammed her sweet face through the windshield. Or an airliner had gone down. Hey, who calls you then? Somebody at the other end of an 800-number?

"Relax," whispered Marilyn.

The phone rang again—louder.

"Shh," she murmured, and shifted her weight on his groin.

"*Uff da*," said Strether and lay there pinned beneath her, a pillow propped behind his head. Over the lampshade hung a red silk scarf. The phone was a cheap plastic device already repaired twice with duct-tape.

(If you missed Strether's Editor's Column, you can turn back to page 11.)

When it rang again, he could see the thing jangle, threatening—out of spite—to fly apart into jagged pieces.

"Mmm," said Marilyn, her hair falling like a curtain about his face.

"I'd better see who it is," he said.

"Hush," she said.

"It might be important."

"Wrong number," she whispered, her breath coming hot in his ear.

Strether eased back and tried to think, tried to re-assemble his identity. Who was he—in this body, in this dark wood, this crummy apartment? Okay, he decided. His mother was already dead. And his father got pretty good care in a nursing home out near <u>Southdale</u>.[1] So who'd call about <u>Hester</u>.[2], Still, he had this feeling—of something dark rushing past that he ought to reach out and seize, or maybe halt. Lately signs were presenting themselves, like mute voices begging to be deciphered. At the edge of sleep, unearthly lips brushed his ear, whispering ghastly syllables. Let go, <u>they seemed to say.</u>[3]

He shot out a hand. It caught the phone on what he figured was the last ring.

------

[1] A shopping mall in Edina, a southwest Minneapolis suburb.

Oh!" cried Marilyn, as the quilt slid them both off the bed.

"Hello?" he said, hitting the floor.

"Arthur Strether? This is <u>Margo Caxton.</u>[4] Remember me?"

"<u>How could I forget," he said.</u>[5]

On the floor, Marilyn clung to Strether and pressed one ear to his chest, as if listening to something at the interior. Then she got up and padded off to the bathroom. She was a nice young woman—not exactly an intel-lectual—who ran a cash register at the hardware store. One steamy afternoon in the warehouse,

Violence, Masochism, & Poise in the Classics

Cultural History as you've never heard it before.

An extraordinary audio- cassette presentation by one of America's most elec-trifying college professors. Thousands of men and women have impressed their friends with their knowledge of Classical Violence and Masochism after hearing Prof. Gildersleeve Hilderstrom's dynamic lec-tures. See our Web-site for further details.

---

[4] The Pulitzer Prize-winning poet, a lovely charming woman—married to the other well-known Caxton, the literary editor.

[5] She had shown up in December to hear him read a paper on Longfellow at the MLA convention. She had actually asked for a copy to show her husband for possible publication. They'd had a nice chat making their way through the crowd, and then were swept into an elevator—packed in so tight that the other delegates couldn't angle glances at each other's con-vention name-badges. He felt her soft haunch pressed tight against his groin, and he took in lungfuls of her scent: *Coco Chanel.*

she'd dared him to make his move. So he J7d1 her—on a pile of Sacrete Mortar Mix. Where was the true value in that?

"Are you there, Strether?" said the voice on the phone.

"Of course," he said. "This is about that paper on Longfellow, right?"

"No. This is about *you*."

"Really." He took a breath. Was this attractive older woman calling him from 2,000 miles away because he'd had an erection in an elevator?

"Did you get that job you interviewed for at the MLA?"

"Not exactly," he said.[6]

"So you're free—to come out here to Oregon?"

Gosh. What did she have in mind? Flying him out for a quicky?

"Oh dear," she said. "I forgot to tell you. Bill wants you to come out and work for the magazine—and have a good look at you."

Having a *good look* sounded like something Strether's mother would have said. And did her ghostly presence account for his vaguely erotic interest in older women— was it some Freudian fixation?

His mom was always old and eccentric. She'd had a brilliant career as a teacher, had many men and women friends—probably some were lovers.

---

[6] These days, departments of English weren't interested in candidates over forty who displayed lapses of attention, fits of irritability, and suffered from auditory hallucinations. Which is why he was working in a hardware store.

In her late forties she finally married Strether's father, an engineer. By the time Strether was in junior high school, she was in her sixties, wore her husband's old khaki pants and T-shirts around the house, often forgot to comb her hair or where she'd set down her false-teeth. You couldn't expect a kid to see the humor when clerks in stores assumed she was his grandmother. Still, at math, real estate, and bullying used car salesmen, she was a genius.

She loved to drive, but she pressed too hard on the gas, then on the brakes, to coast in an inner reverie. Sitting in the front seat of the old Ford Galaxy beside her, one was thrown forward and back as she lurched and plunged her vehicle down roadways.

This style of driving once led to an unusual incident. Strether's older sister had taken up the project of wallpapering. This seemed like a foolhardy idea. They knew from movies and TV that wallpaper was full of comic surprises: high ladders could tip, pots of paste might end up on someone's head, gooey rolls would unfurl and engulf an incompetent paperhanger. Massive wet tangles always muffled the cries of these flailing victims.

Still, she rented an old wallpaper steamer—a contraption with a hose that heated water and pumped up pressure above a kerosene burner. Her mother told her to exercise *extreme caution* (the same phrase she employed when hinting at the issue of pre-marital sex), then drove off with Strether to run errands. But after half an hour, nagging worries made her circle back through their neighborhood to see if the house was on fire.

Their house was second from the corner, so crossing the avenue she peered back—oh, merely for a quick look. Just then, his sister barged out the front door, down the steps, and around the corner of the house. She'd finished stripping a bedroom wall and wanted a view of her work from outside, through the window. She'd do the same thing after putting lights on the Christmas tree.

But Strether's mother, certain her daughter was fleeing an inferno, hit the brakes. A hard bump threw them back as someone rear-ended them.

Neither were aware that a frowning man in a business suit had been tailing them for several blocks, trying—the

the best he could—to match the lurching rhythm of gas pedal, brake, coast. Now suddenly the driver ahead of him had screeched to a stop in the middle of a deserted residential intersection.

The gentleman leaned out his window looking rattled. Next he evidently saw a wild-looking creature emerge from the car ahead. Baggy pants, sagging breasts filling a dirty T-shirt, wild gray hair flying in all directions, it came at him, a horrible gaping hole for a mouth as it hollered, "The wallpaper! The wallpaper!" He clutched the wheel, half-closed his eyes, and whispered something to himself as the horrid thing dashed up the sidewalk.

Strether watched his mom hurry toward the house, then went around to shut the driver's-side door. In all directions, the streets were deserted. He inspected the rear bumper of the sturdy Ford Galaxy, then approached the other driver.

The man sat staring ahead, visibly shaken.

"I don't see any damage here," said Strether. "And the wallpaper is off."

"Is that *good*?" The man was pleading for an answer to ultimate questions.

"That was the plan. I think you can be on your way."

"Ah, *the Plan*. Bless you," said the fellow, backed up and had driven off.

Now Marilyn came back from the bathroom, Strether had hung up the phone. He'd accepted the Caxton's offer, agreeing to move his household to the west coast for six months. By "household," he meant his bed and night stand, one aluminum lawn chair, a second-hand sofa, an old computer, some tools, and his books. The books, still in cartons from his <u>last move</u>,[7] were stacked up in the hallway from <u>the move before last</u>. [8]

Marilyn was putting on her bra, looking confused and

Make Big Bucks Publishing in Small Literary Magazines: an Insider's Guide

"Serves up the perfect recipe for poets and writers—who *dare* to *take risks*."

— Korkus Reviews

Let master editor and scholar, Wynk de Worde, share his time-tested secrets for moving from the slush-pile to early retirement in Maui.

This 8-page pamphlet is now available in plain brown wrapper from AQR, 776 Atrium Place, Vanport, Cascadia. $39.95 plus $5.05 Postage & Handling.

Cultural Studies in 19th-century American Literature at Vanport State University. Sept. 20th- 23rd, 2001.
Send MS. to Arthur Strether c/o AQR 776 Atrium Place, Vanport, Cascadia.

hurt, as if someone had made off with her clothes. "I don't have to put up with this shit," she said.

Strether was staring at the phone, picturing not his mom, but his dad in his wheelchair, grim and silent. How to break the news—about leaving town—to him? When Strether had shown up, unemployed, at the nursing home in January, the old guy must have thought that his son had finally come home to take care of him. But Minneapolis had changed so much over the years that Strether hardly recognized the place. Maybe he could move <u>his dad out to Oregon?</u> [9]

A vision appeared of the land rolling west across of the Dakotas and Montana—Interstate 90 climbing into the Rockies (probably snow still in the passes), the highway running flat across the barren eastern half of Washington state. Gosh, how many miles?

He glanced up at Marilyn. The sight of her fine hair, damply matted across her forehead, evoked a great sadness in him. Her hair smelled so

sweet. It was some chemical, maybe methylisothia-

---

[9] The editor has deleted this long footnote—calling it "wordy." You may consult it in the *AQR* Archives, p. 223ff.

olinone, an ingredient in her shampoo. Minutes ago, they'd been adrift in another zone, coursing through warm tides toward some secret, verdant shore. He'd almost made it—to this new place he was after. Something to do with the Spirit, with Woman, the ungraspable essence.

"Marilyn, do you know that I've grown fond of you?"

She got up on one elbow. "How come you keep calling me Marilyn? My name is Marilee."

She pulled away and stared at him. "Who was that on the phone?"

He spotted his jockey shorts on the floor and did the math: Minneapolis to Oregon, say, 2,000 miles. Divide by 50. Forty hours of driving time.

"When I was in the bathroom," said Marilee, "I heard you say something about renting a truck?"

"Well," he said. "Probably 48 hours in a truck."

"Oh hell!" She got out of bed, picked up her bra, and put it on. "You promised you'd quit that. At a time like this, you're adding up numbers!"

Her riled expression reminded him of the look on the faces of certain house cats he'd offended—usually Siamese—before they lashed out. So now what had he done? She was upset, and he hated that.

Marilee thrust her arms through the sleeves of her pink sweater. "You drive me nuts," she declared, "with all your little goals with numbers attached. Like I told you, you're gonna have a heart attack."

"You told me that?"

"Yeah, you're the type. The heart attack type. For one thing, you got an arrhythmia. Listen to your chest some time. And quit worrying about what time it is, or answering the phone. You ever noticed how you jump when the phone rings? That's another sign."

Strether watched as she stepped into her skirt. "How do you know all about heart attacks?"

"I read a magazine article. At the dentist's office." She pointed at the seat of his aluminum lawn chair. "Look. It's worn out on the front edge."

Strether got up to look.

"A famous case," she declared. "An upholsterer discovered that in the waiting room of a couple of cardiologists, Friedman and Rosenman. Heart attack types always sit on the edge of their chairs." Marilee slung her purse over her shoulder. "Well? I guess this is it, huh?"

"Tell me something." he said. "Where are you going?"

"I'm getting out of here before you drive me nuts."

"Just because I sit on the edge of my chair?"

"Cut the bullshit, Strether. The phone rings and all of a sudden you're telling me how fond you are of me. I'm not an idiot. Why don't you just say you're leaving town? It's a college job isn't it? Probably some high-class place with ivy on the walls, rich sorority girls following you around—" Marilee was close to tears.

If Strether had pants on, he would have put his hands in his pockets.

"Guys like you—" She snatched the red scarf off the lampshade. Around the scarf's edge they'd threaded little beads, like lead sinkers. Marilee stretched the fabric taut and whipped it out. "You're a curse on womankind!"

she shrieked, flailing Strether about the head and shoulders. He put up his hands and winced, feeling the sting of those little beads drawing blood. Where would she strike next?

"You always had an excellent imagination," said a voice. Strether wheeled about to face a stout, gray-haired woman. She stood at the foot of the bed wearing a ragged T-shirt, janitor pants, and tennis shoes with the toes cut out.

"Aw, Ma," he said. Lately his mother's ghost had been appearing—to save him from going crazy.

She held up a finger of admonition. "Don't say anything you wouldn't want printed on the front page of the *Lanesboro Leader*." Good advice, but hard to apply to the present situation.

"Guys like you—"she said, snatching the red scarf off the lampshade. It was silky and soft in her hands.

["The Calling" continued on p. 43]

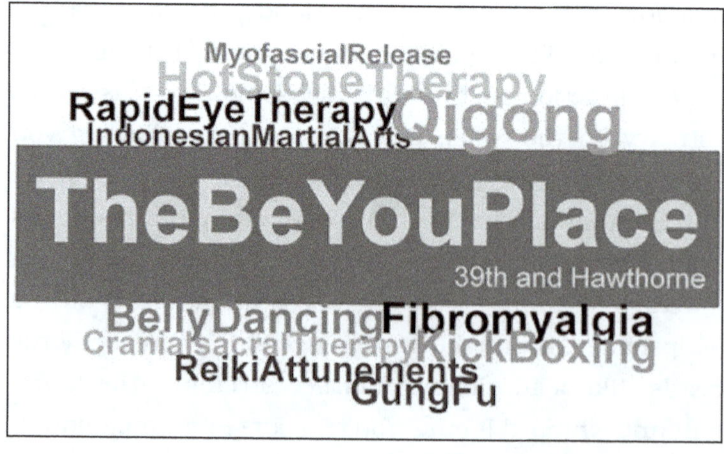

Daddy?
an Investigative Report

Zolar Zapf
explores certain irregularities in
Sylvia Plath's birth certificate.

Beside the entrance of 23 Fitzroy Road — the house where Sylvia Plath committed suicide—hangs one of those blue historical markers familiar to anyone who has walked the streets of literary London.

The fact that Yeats "lived here" strikes one critic as "oddly irrelevant,"[1] perhaps because the Irish poet arrived there as a toddler and left when he was seven.[2]

Yet three months before Plath's death, the sight of this blue plaque provoked a dash up the stairs when she spotted a "Flat To Let" sign posted outside of the London townhouse. In a letter to her mother, she claims the spirit of Yeats had touched her when she visited his tower in Ireland.[3] She's referring to a  visit she made to Ballylee—with Ted Hughs, just before their separation—in September, 1962.

The influence of Yeats on Plath has been explored by a number of critics, especially Sandra Gilbert.[4] She notes that a poem (Matthew Arnold's "The Forsaken Merman," in which a woman seduces and abandons a poet) read aloud by Plath's mother, Aurelia, must have been a formative influence. But the role Yeats played in the life of Aurelia Schober Plath has never been explored.

---

[1] See Janet Malcolm, "The Silent Woman," in *The New Yorker*, 23 & 30 Aug, 1993, p. 107.

[2] A. Norman Jeffares, *W. B. Yeats: a New Biography* (London: Hutchinson, 1988), pp. 4-5.

[3] Sylvia Plath, *Letters Home*, ed. Aurelia Schober Plath (New York: Harper & Row, 1975), p. 480.

[4] Sandra M. Gilbert, "In Yeats' House: The Death and Resurrection of Sylvia Plath," in Linda Wagner, *Critical Essays on Sylvia Plath* (Boston, 1982), pp.204-22.

Deep in Indiana University's Plath Archives[5] is a curious object, acquired in 1977 from an American book dealer: Aurelia Plath's personal copy of *The Oxford Anthology of English Poetry*.[6] The hefty volume surveys major poets—roughly from Chaucer to Dylan Thomas. Here and there, mostly among the Victorian and Modern poets, one finds her marginal notations. The Arnold poem, for example, has a few words underlined.

Sylvia's mother has gone over several Yeats poems making small checks—occasionally exclamation points— in the margins. Now, what comes next is very peculiar. The last stanza of Yeats' famous poem, "Crazy Jane Talks to the Bishop," has been crossed out. At the bottom of the page, the following (perhaps a variant version of the stanza?) is neatly printed in her hand:

> *A woman can be proud and stiff*
> *Entangled in love's snare;*
> *But Love has pitched his mansion in*
> *This circled monolith;*
> *The careless swoon of spired hair:*
> *Enforced love of another.*
>
> 　　　*— recited across river from*
> 　　　　*Oregon—Jan 1, 1933*

What do we make of this curiosity?

Manuscripts of the poem reveal that Yeats was satisfied with its final, published, form in November of 1931.[7] Still, it would not appear in print until the publication of *The Winding Stair and*

---

[5] Plath MSS. II, Box 13: (Memorabilia, Cambridge and Teaching Year at Smith).

[6] New York: Oxford Univ. Press, 1956.

[7] See W. B. Yeats, *Words for Music Perhaps and Other Poems*: Manuscript Materials, ed. David R. Clark (Ithaca, Cornell Univ. Press), p. 573.

Other Poems (1933). So in early 1933, the poet could have been considering last-minute revisions.

But where was Yeats in January 1933? Why, in New York! At least a letter, postmarked from the Waldorf Astoria, suggests that location.[8]

The poet embarked on his second American tour October 22, 1932, and was back in England on January 28, 1933 (Jeffares, 310). He'd attended seances in Boston, and gave readings in New York, Boston, Detroit, and Toronto. Aurelia mights have heard him recite a poem in Boston—except that according to records she ostensibly had an infant to care for. (Sylvia's birth certificate is dated October 27, 1932. More about this document—also in the Lilly archives—later.)

Aurelia's version of the "Crazy Jane" stanza also bore a location: "Oregon"? On a whim, I checked Portland's *Oregonian* on microfilm and found the following extraordinary 1933 news item.

The photo caption caught my eye immediately.

---

[8] See Allan Wade, *Letters of W. B. Yeats* (London, Macmillan: 1955), p. 803-4.

GOLDEN [...] **TY ACCORDS CELEBRITY AND TRAVE** [...] **MPANION A ROUSING SEND-OFF**

The scene at Portland's train depot was a bit mysterious—both hush-hush and a glittering social occasion for those in the know. The visiting celebrity — who asked not to be named—had delighted a large audience the other evening reading from his new book. His companion, Miss Schobe, seemed a-flutter at the attention lavished upon her. The two greeted the New Year in Goldendale Washington, at the home of the late, Sam Hill. Seances and astronomical observations were among the rumored festivities, which surely must must have included a visit to Hill's War Memorial. The unexpected and charming visitors to Portland left by private car for undisclosed points to the East. Bon Voyage!

The original "Golden Dawn," in the 1890's, was a secret society into which Yeats was initiated by Samuel Mathers—the eccentric Rosicrucian who would later take Aleister Crowley as his protege. But Portland's 1933 "Golden Dawn" seems merely a club for socialites. A familiar face leans in toward "Miss Schobe." (Aurelia's maiden name was Schober.) The "private cars" may have been those provided by Henry Ford in all major cities Yeats visited.

But most curious is the reference to Hill's "War Memorial." See the map below for a bit of geography.

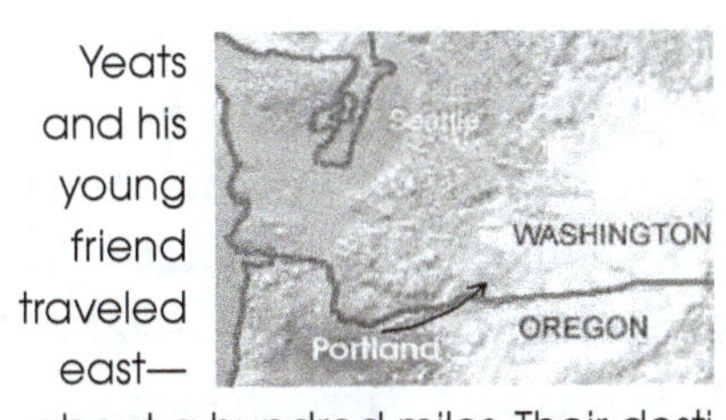

Yeats and his young friend traveled east— about a hundred miles. Their destination was a monument set up above the Columbia River where it cuts through the high desert.

In 1918, Sam Hill (eccentric road builder, millionaire, and hanger-on with royalty) began constructing his full-size replica of Stonehenge—as it must have looked in 1500 BC. He completed the project—dedicated to soldiers killed in World War I—in 1929. Oddly, some still think the site's existence is a myth.

Through his international occult contacts, Hill implored Yeats to visit Maryhill—as he named it. But Hill died in 1931, while Yeats was planning his American tour.

If Stonehenge, even in replica, was designed to track solar and lunar events (solstices, eclipses), we can see how Yeats and Miss Schober may have engaged in

Sam Hill: Collection of The Maryhill Museum of Art

"astronomical observations" at a "War Memorial."

Now we're prepared to look again at the variant "Crazy Jane" poem. And to fill in the links between events at Maryhill and Sylvia Plath's birth certificate. Of course, Maryhill itself is a far more important topic than Plath's poetry or parentage.

Yes, they told me that an interview below might get inserted at this point in my argument. Shucks, what the French call *le discourse des sound-bites* don't quite line up with the lingo of scholarship, does it? Okay, let's get this Plath business out of the way, pronto. Here's that variant stanza again:

> A woman can be proud and stiff
> Entangled in love's snare;
> But Love has pitched his mansion in
> This circled monolith;
> The careless swoon of spired hair:
> Enforced love of another.

Sounds to me like an erotic seduction orchestrated within a dramatic setting: the "circled monolith" of a Stonehenge replica. (You wouldn't believe what it takes sometimes for an old fellow to get laid.)

The rest is pretty obvious. Yeats Jʌʤ Aurelia at Maryhill, the kid was born 9 months later (about September, 1933), and records changed to hide the whole sorry business. I've had my staff examine the photostat birth certificate, manipulate it under ultraviolet and Adobe Photoshop,® and set forth the results here for your inspection.

<table>
<tr><td>_____ Sylvia Plath _____</td><td>weighing 6 ___ lbs. ___ 9 __ ozs.</td></tr>
<tr><td>·n in this hospital at______</td><td>2:10 _______ o'clock __ P·.m.</td></tr>
<tr><td>_____________ day of______</td><td>______________ 19 33</td></tr>
<tr><td colspan="2">ss Whereof, the said Hospital has
his Certificate to be signed by its</td></tr>
</table>

In the *Literary News* today, scholar and adventurer, Zolar Zapf claims that Sylvia Plath's birth certificate was altered. In an interview, we asked him how his findings would influence Plath studies. "I don't give a damn about Sylvia Plath" he said.

So, at the age of 67, the old poet <u>fathered a bastard</u>. After New Year's, Aurelia high-tailed it to Reno Nevada where her other lover, Otto Plath, was establishing his six-week residency for a <u>quicky divorce</u>.*

Now, back to our real business: the moon at Maryhill. On New Year's Eve 1932, the moon was entering Pisces barely three days past new. Curiously Yeats supplies the phrase, "Enforced love of another," to this phase of the lunar cycle.[9] Now, if the pair had hoped to view the mildly spectacular occur-

---

* The biography, of course, claims this divorce was granted exactly one year earlier. And—wouldn't you know it?—the original Nevada divorce and marriage records for the 1930's were destroyed by the Carson City fire of 1953. But the ledger at Washoe Pines Ranch (it catered to those seeking to establish residency—they were mostly women, for example, Mirna Loy) shows that one "O. Emil Plath" paid his 6-week bill in full on Jan. 2, 1933—in time to marry the now pregnant Miss Schober on January 4th. I leave the job of investigating subsequent irregularities—Sylvia's entry to school a year early, etc.—to Plath scholars.

By the way, Yeats underwent the Steinach operation—which was actually a vasectomy, not a transplanting of monkey glands—in the Spring of 1933. [See V. Pruitt's useful article, "Yeats & the Steinach Operation" in *American Imago*, 34 (Fall, 1977): 287-96.]

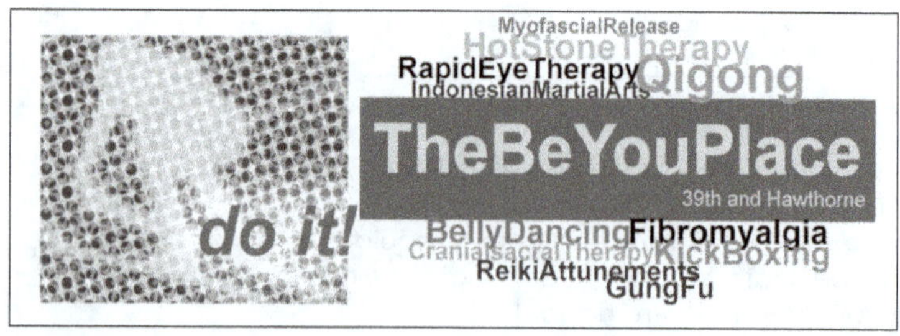

rence of the moon setting over Mt. Hood to the west, they might have been disappointed—for this is the mid-summer alignment. [10]

I've found that most people don't pay much attention to the moon. Now and then I ask them, "What time of day does the Full Moon rise?" They don't know it's at sunset! Find somebody looking up at the moon. Ask them, "Where—at this same time—will it be tomorrow night?" They'll shrug. Spread your fingers and hold them, at arm's length, up to the sky. Tell them, "13 degrees to the east." Have they noticed that the moon, in winter, rides high in the sky like the summer sun? Nope.

So, on New Year's Eve, Yeats and Aurelia surely would have glimpsed, off in the northwest, *The New Moon Holding the Old Moon in its Arms.*

There's an old song about the new moon. It links the immutable to the transient in human affairs. Aw, what the hell. Mind if <u>I reach for my guitar?</u>

----

[10] See W. B. Ernest Piini's useful diagram in *America's Stonehenge* (Sarsen Press: Redwood CA, 1980), p.9.

Hemingway, Gertrude Stein, and the Art of the Sestina

Literary Analysis by Georges Auriol

We imagine that conversation at 27 rue de Fleurus in the twenties was brilliant. Yet I know of only one attempt to capture, on the page, the sizzle and snap of expatriate repartee. The scene appears in an unusual poem by Isaac Moore. Few have pushed the taut constraints of the sestina to such extremes. Accordingly, a quick review of the sestina's form is in order.

[continued on p. 113.]

["The Calling" continued from page 32}

"You're a curse on woman-kind." She stuffed the scarf in her purse.

The bright light bulb made Strether wince. What a terrible thing to be accused of, he thought, watching his mother's figure dissolve and fade to black. "I was going to ask your advice," he told Marilee. "About leaving. When the time was right."

"Yeah, sure." She headed for the door.

He bowed his head, penitent, and searched for appropriate words. "Listen, I know you want me to *lighten up*—as you'd put it. And I'm trying to *get a life*. But it's all new for me. There are rules here, unwritten codes, even matters of diction, that I find perplexing. You can imagine how stressful it is, being with a younger woman, engaging in sex, romance—"

She came back and faced him. "Don't joke with me. This ain't romance."

"I'm not joking. I'm serious. Maybe I should give it up."

"Oh yeah?"

"It's not healthy. Especially sex. I'll just quit."

"Oh yeah? I dare you."

From the night stand, she snatched a black hardbound volume. "Swear on the *Bible*," she said.

"Swear? Come on." Should he tell her she was holding the Oxford edition of Fowler's *Modern English Usage*? "Okay," he said, and put his hand on the book.

"No more J7dıℓ, right?"

"None?"

"Yeah, for— Oh, a year."

"That long?"

"Hurry up, or I'll make it two."

"Okay," he said, thinking his mother—wherever she was—might approve. I'll remain chaste for—"

"Chased? Don't put in any loopholes."

"Whatever you say, I swear," he said.

"This is so stupid," she said and tossed the book aside.

Strether felt peculiar—lightheaded.

Marilee stood there, biting her lovely lip, searching his face with moist eyes. Would she kiss him good-bye? Nope, she wasn't a fool. She walked out, slamming the door. Against the wall, his ancient KLH record player rattled on its wooden orange crate. They didn't make those crates anymore.

Strether felt an old ache in his heart. He put his hand on Fowler's *English Usage* again and thought he felt an electric tingle shoot up his arm. He hefted the book. It represented usage, the word, a system of signs. Gosh, he used to love it. And professed to know how to teach it. And hey, his old love, teaching, demanded a kind of chastity—especially when it came to female students. Somewhere a college would want him back. Wasn't it his true vocation, his calling?

And then—abruptly—Strether wept. A great weight forced him to his knees. The bitter years battered him down. In his throat rose a great round vowel of remorse, and he moaned for the dead, for those he'd wronged, for the mess he'd made of his life.

Fiction

The Victim

by
Robert Granjon

Last week, Edna Johnson—a Twin Cities widow in her sixties—had a very unusual experience. She'd taken the bus downtown. At 10:00 A.M. on the 5th floor of a major Minneapolis department store, she visited the Ladies' rest room. Snapping the lock shut in a stall, Edna set her purse down on the clean tile floor, hefted up her blue rayon skirt, slid down her—

Suddenly a hand darted in at her feet. It snatched her purse! Just like that. Edna yelled and tugged up her panty-hose. As she burst out of the rest room, two people in line at Customer Service stared in her direction. They saw a well-dressed senior citizen, eyes wild with indignation.

"Thief! Thief!" cried Edna.

A woman escorted her up to the business offices, where a receptionist dialed Security. "Was it a man or a woman?" they asked.

"A man?" said Edna. In the Ladies' rest room?

A form was filled out. For insurance purposes, they said. Then a polite gentleman with a walkie-talkie took her down an elevator, out the door, and put her in a taxi-cab. He slipped her a twenty-dollar bill for the fare back to suburban Edina.

When the cab circled up her driveway, Edna sensed neighbors watching as she handed the driver a big tip. Around back, she found the spare key to the front door. Her late husband, Hubert, had fashioned a little secret door in an outdoor light-switch to hide the key. They'd bought this house the year he retired. That winter, he climbed up to shovel heavy snow off the roof and suffered a fatal heart attack. Edna found it difficult to believe he was gone. She went out and stood on the lawn to survey the roof. She went from room to room whispering. She stared at his favorite armchair, examined his books—still on the shelves.

Edna's daughter finally insisted they donate all the furniture—all the old memories—to the Salvation Army. With insurance money, she and Edna made extravagant trips to Ethan Allen. They picked out Chippendale sofas and Queen Anne arm chairs, tea-tables and low-boys; curio-cabinets, consoles, and commodes; china cabinets with leaded glass windows and apothecary chests with brass pulls; butler's-tray-tables, drop-leaf-tables, pedestal-tables; a four-post canopy bed, a lady's writing desk, an armoire, dressers with mirrors: an entire houseful of brand-new furniture for an old lady.

It was noon when Edna turned the key in the front door. Inside, the big hallway clock struck the hour. She kicked off her shoes and flopped down on a couch. Light streamed in high windows onto tufted upholstery and varnished wood. Then the phone rang. A man said they'd found her purse. Yes, her checkbook, credit cards, birthday book—nothing seemed to be missing. Could she come down to the store and identify it?

"Thank goodness," she said. Her bus ride downtown seemed unusual. Circling past Lake Calhoun, she noticed the thick foliage of maples and oaks in Lakewood Cemetery. On Hennepin Avenue, she saw a mother pushing a shiny baby-carriage past a brilliantly revolving barber-pole. Nicollet Mall bustled with lunch-hour gaiety. At intersections, the stop lights glowed the delicious red of wild-cherry Life-Savers.

Edna felt light-headed as she rode the department store's escalator up to the business offices. The receptionist was getting ready to go to lunch.

"Well, here I am again," said Edna.

The receptionist looked at her blankly.

"You called. Someone called about finding my purse?"

The woman dialed Security, spoke a few words, then shook her head. No purse had been found.

"But—" said Edna.

"Hey, I'm sorry," said the woman, getting out her own hand-bag from a locked drawer. "You don't look so hot. Sit down and take it easy. Then go home and take a nice cool shower. Really."

Edna's third bus ride was an ordeal. "Hubert?" she whispered, sitting on a broken seat as the vehicle lurched through traffic. Exhaust fumes came in a window she couldn't slide shut.

Trudging up her driveway, she heard a voice call her name. It was Alice from next door, going on about someone's house up for sale. Edna ignored her neighbor. Edna was staring at deep wheel ruts in her front lawn.

"I didn't expect to see you again," Alice was saying. "Look I brought my camera."

Edna fumbled in a pocket for the spare key. Oddly, the front screen-door yawned wide-open, propped there with a big book. It looked like Hubert's unabridged dictionary.

"And those fellows worked so fast," said Alice, "I wondered if maybe you'd died or something."

"Fellows?" said Edna, going up the steps, key in hand.

"The movers. The ones with the U-Haul van. Why didn't you tell me you were selling the house? Listen, I want to take a snap-shot."

Edna tried the door. It was securely locked.

"I could have helped pack," said Alice.

"Goodness, they were careless, those men. I saw them drop your new grandfather clock. They loaded that big truck in a jiffy."

"A big truck?" said Edna. Delirious, she concentrated on fitting the key into the lock. As she pushed the heavy door open—just a crack—it happened. A very unusual experience. First a bright flash of light. Then a wonderful clarity descended. She felt suspended—calm and airy—weightless in a region of warm wind. What lay past that doorway? Probably broken glass on bare floors, echoing empty rooms. But Edna didn't move. And she didn't look back.

Instead she hung there—impossibly frozen, as in a snapshot—adrift in a thin zone, the stuff of thresholds, narrow as a thickness of glass.   ■

Newcomer falls into state

#1 Searching for Margo

Serial fiction by Anton Garamond

EPISODE 1: In this first episode, Luke Waxman—an unemployed and over-educated midwesterner—finds himself sleepless, on a strange mission to Portland.:

Streaking downhill toward Yakima in a rented, yellow, Riter truck, Luke Waxman wondered if he was under attack. On a ridge to the east, artillery shells exploded in puffs of black smoke. The signs along this western highway said, "Military Firing Range." But he was a little paranoid after driving all night. Usually it was the IRS on his tail—not the U.S. Army.

He'd be safe, back in Minnesota if it wasn't for Olga. She'd died last week in a horrible coughing fit. Lovely Olga of the Earth Mother hips. Preferring women to men, she'd spurned him, then lay there on her deathbed and made him promise.

"Take this Hag's Ring," she whispered. "Give it to—*her*. Then tell her what you think women really want Get it wrong, she'll cut off your wiener."

Luke found this hard to believe. But okay, this other woman, *Margo*, lived in Oregon—of all places. To humor poor Olga, he accepted the ring. She believed in a lot of zany magic. Since he'd lost his job, his car, he flipped a coin. It told him to rent a truck, go west, and get a life.

Now, outside Yakima, Luke saw Jeeps full of guys in camouflage. Some were women. They lined the shoulder of U.S. 97 and glared at him—as if his truck was the target they'd missed. His map

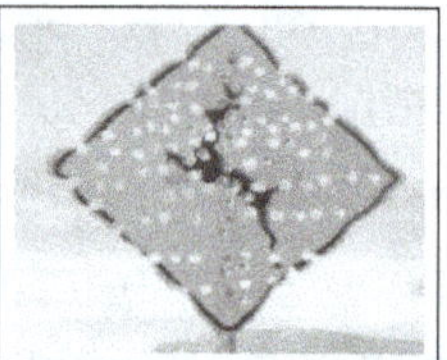

said this wasteland was a big Indian Reservation. Was the
government taking it back?

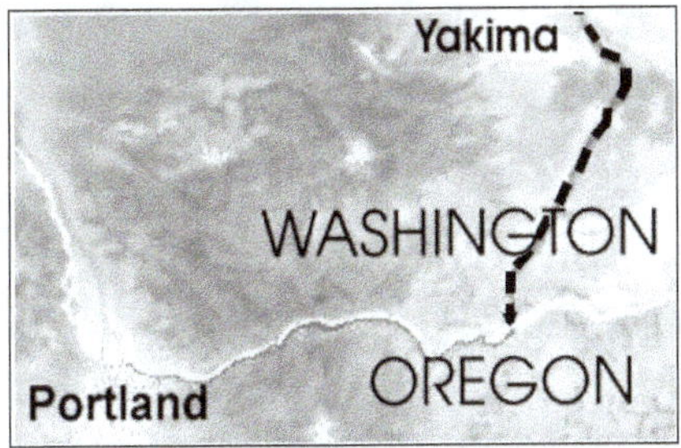

Luke saw a woman
firing her M-16 at a
Deer Crossing sign.
When she was done it
looked like a device for
draining spaghetti.

So this was *The
West.* Before yester-
day, he'd never been
past Fargo. But he knew what to expect. Bullet holes in the
road signs. In Portland, everybody wore Timberline boots
and plaid shirts.

Now fatigue took over. The rented truck strained up
hills, then raced him down into wooded valleys. He gripped
the wheel and got into the rhythm of it, felt his mind float
free to hover outside the body. He observed dull fingers
cramped into claws, allowed bone and flesh to melt into
numbness.

He decided he had x-ray vision. It was possible. Below
the concrete, aggregate lay rolled to government specifica-
tions. Particles shifted in the voids. Overhead the hum of
rubber hung in the air like Sanskrit syllables.

In the mountains of Tibet they call this *Ham Sah:* min-
eral self-awareness. And now Luke understood that the
true function of any long highway drive was to become a
meditational exercise.

Sit erect. Ignore the temperature gauge edging the red
line. The world wanted only to shackle him to desire. Sure
enough: "Chain Up Lane 1,000 feet." Observe phantom
foot...

"Oh Jeez!" he cried, pumping the brakes. He was coast-
ing down a steep hill. Had he come this far only to drown,
mangled but illuminated, in the Columbia River? He
hollered all the way down.

[continued on page 80]

[Continued from p. 16.]

The Editor's Column Part II

Art Strether

Over the next few days, I settled into Bill Caxton's empty office. Ignoring all his unanswered mail, I've revised the shape of my Longfellow article.

You wonder, perhaps, at me rambling on like this. Ever since the murder in the house, they've all gone off somewhere. Wynk has shut me in a room to fill blank pages in the new issue. I have no doubt that someone will edit this sophomoric typing before anyone reads it. In which case... Anything is permitted! Gosh, what paradoxes we inhabit.

At any rate, Bill Caxton has disappeared—left town. We face a frantic deadline to get first this ragtag digital issue out, and some events have shaken my confidence in the entire venture. For example, Wynk insists we employ a certain obscure software platform he purchased—at an exorbitant cost, with technical support that never seem to answer their phones—from an obscure dot-com in Modesto

California. He incurs obscene charges telephoning for technical advice to fix bugs in the system. Peculiar things happen on my own screen—but then, tired eyes can't always be trusted. I haven't slept well lately, flinging off the succubi astride my chest. It's rather like dialing fantasy hotlines, hoping they'll do the talking. But let me describe one run in with a grotesque woman whose story I rejected. She had a big voice, one of those peculiar moments that strike this system: lines of text go crazy, some kind of electrical interference intrudes upon our layouts. Signs in the static?

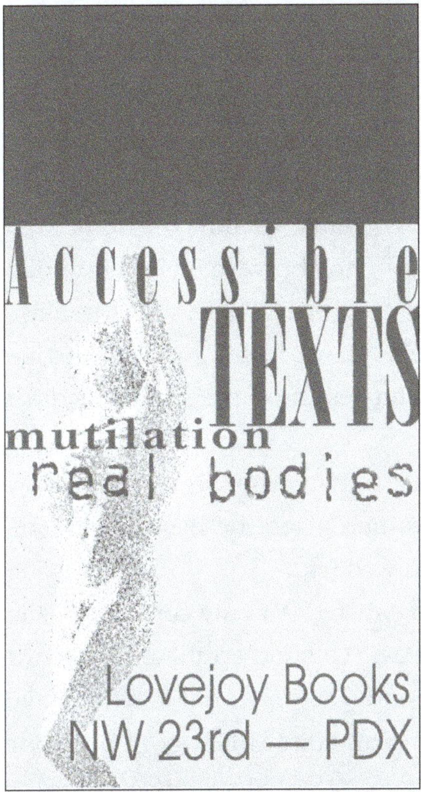

The subject came up during our first meeting. Wearing his blue blazer, Wynk had pulled me aside on the crowded deck during a cocktail party for donors.

Wynk de Worde is an intense fellow, about my height, with a close cropped beard. There's a sarcastic slant to his mouth, and he looks— Well, he never removes those preposterous dark glasses.

"Okay, Strether," he said. "You probably want to know which of these young women gives the best blows jobs to editors and published writers.

I looked at him, feeling stung. Was my condition—my erotic neediness mingled with a spotty publishing record —so obvious? Needless to say, I would hardly have phrased the perogatives of an editor his way. "I beg your pardon?"

"Which one of these women can we lay off first?" he said. The yellow Lab come over and sniffed his hand.

"Oh, that's surely Caxton's concern, isn't it?"

"Hey—" Wynk said. "You think I resemble Bill?"

I glanced away from this odd remark to take in the view from the deck. A forested slope descends several miles to the skyline of Portland—and beyond that hovered the misty outline of <u>Mt. Hood</u>. "You mean fire somebody?" I said. "He's probably spent years gathering these people around him. You just can't—"

"Listen," he hissed. "A few cuts add extras to make this magazine *soar.* Hiring the string quartet and band gives us music! For turning pages, right? Like *All Things Considered.* So we got a few bugs in the KurtzView software. I've got a guy fixing it. Marlowe—ha ha."

"You were saying—about laying off staff?"

"Oh," he said. "I just handed out pink slips." Wynk ran through <u>a list</u>. He was actually going to fire them.

I was speechless. How could we produce a magazine now?

"Hey, listen," he went on. "We've got big advertising bucks coming in. I'm in touch with General Motors." Behind his dark glasses he seemed to turn inward.

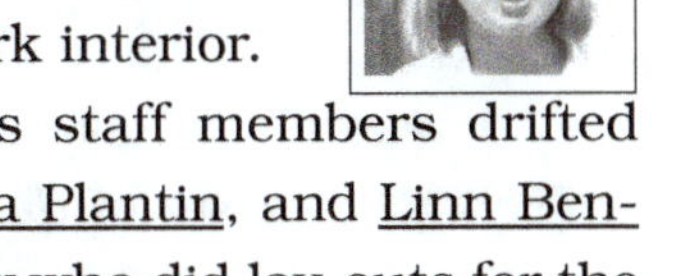

I tried to peer behind those opaque lenses to see some ludicrous irony we could both have a good laugh over. But instead I felt a chill, as if a weird wind was blowing out of a madman's dark interior.

Just then three remainings staff members drifted past: <u>William Caslon</u>, <u>Christina Plantin</u>, and <u>Linn Benton</u>. Caslon was a British fellow who did lay-outs for the magazine. Bernice had an M.A. in Comp. Lit, did copy-editing, and had a high fragile laugh. Lola was wearing a blue top, white shorts, and running shoes. Lola was luscious.

Trailing them came an older fellow in a too-tight bus-boy jacket who shoved a tray of smoked oysters in my face. He had a jaw of granite and a scar on his low forehead. When Wynk and I declined his offer, he clomped away.

"Who's that?" I asked.

"Oh," said Wynk. "That's Culligan, Sable's houseboy."

I recognized Sable's name: Caxton's old friend who'd hired the detective. I watched Culligan, in dirty jeans and steel-toed boots, disappear into the cool house. "That guy is no houseboy," I said. "What's he doing here?"

"Loren lets him hang around. You've met Loren, Sable's wife? A blond, into Astral Imaging—looks like a faded Hollywood starlet?"

"Ah," I said, recalling the woman napping in a room near my own.

"They live in the house next-door. Come on. I'll show you their pool."

We followed a path through the garden, dense with roses. Just then…

…behind us there were gunshots! I listened for a scream, but heard none.

Wynk and I sprinted back to the house. On the patio, everyone was ducking for cover behind canvas deck chairs . <u>Just then</u>…

…we heard a car door slam and someone drive off!

Feeling a spasm of *déjà-vu*, I followed Wynk into the house, through a door, and into the living room.

There stood Loren Sable over a body on the floor. It was Culligan, the house boy. His head was arched back

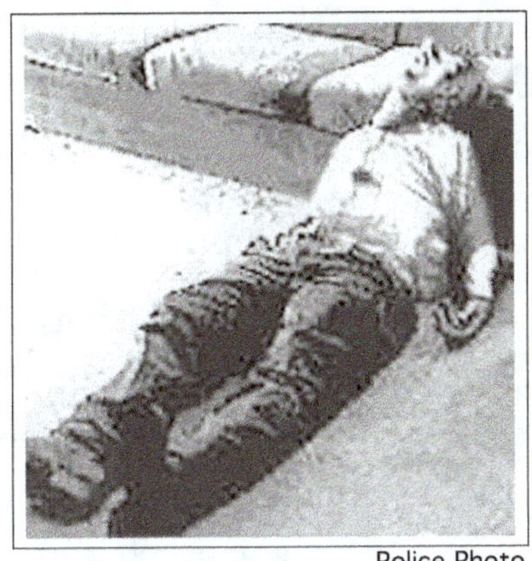
Police Photo

unnaturally on the couch as if to display a nasty exit-wound in his neck. Loren was holding a revolver, gazing at it as if the thing had just materialized from some other astral plane.

"Hold it!" warned a hoarse voice. It was an old geezer with a beard, a rumpled black hat, and a denim jacket. He strode over to Loren and put a careful hand on her shoulder. Taking the revolver by the barrel, he set it on the end table. Dazed Loren sank into a chair. The old guy knelt and felt for a pulse at the dead man's wrist. Then he turned his attention on us.

"Afternoon, Mister de Worde," he said, getting up. "Who's your friend?"

"This is Strether—from the magazine." Wynk sounded shaken, but there was a hint of condescension in his voice.

Behind us, the others were peering in the doorway. At the windows, the faces of curious neighbors appeared.

Caxton stepped in carrying a suitcase. He looked baffled by the sight of a corpse in his living room. "What's happened here, Zapf?"

"Looks like a shooting," said the old guy. "Anybody

know this poor s.o.b?" He gave the dead man's booted toe a nudge with his own.

Then a tall gray-haired man in a rumpled suit appeared—a little out of breath. "My god, it's Culligan!"

Loren stood up, her eyes suddenly full of terror. The tall man took her in his arms, where she shook with sobs.

The room seemed abruptly crowded with strangers. Was that Margo handing out drinks? I looked about, trying to fix details of the scene in memory, but the mass of figures <u>kept shifting</u> and moving about, as if a solid world had entered that inner zone where deceit and desire have their way rearranging the events of the past.

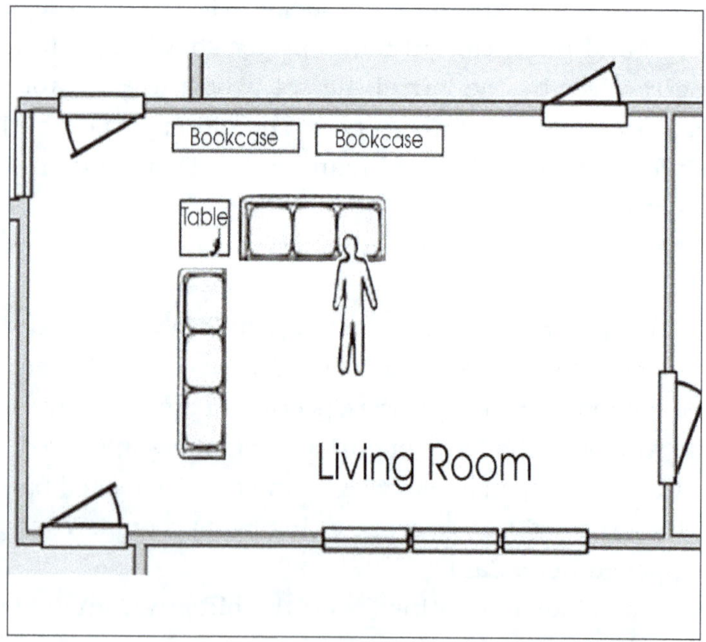

I'd guessed now that the bearded old geezer, called Zapf, was the detective hired by Caxton. They were conferring with the gray-haired man—evidently Gordon Sable, Loren's husband. Given her age, she might have been his third or fourth wife.

Against the rising murmur of voices in the room, I called out: "What about the *car*. We heard a car drive off—after the shots were fired."

Everyone stared at me.

"I didn't hear any car," shrugged Wynk.

Zapf seemed to be examining my large ears, which felt conspicuous. "You two." He pointed to me and Wynk. "Come with me. The rest of you—*stay put*." In the distance the ululating sound of a siren grew louder. Someone had finally called the police.

"Hurry," said Zapf, as he led us out to the garden. We followed the path to Sable's place. "The victim bunked over here. You know where?"

"There's a cottage," said Wynk, who'd stopped. "Past the hedge. But listen—you don't need me. I should be there when the Sheriff arrives."

For an instant, the three of us faced one another in lop-sided triangle. Then Wynk headed back.

Zapf scratched his beard and watched him go. "Rats," he said. "I hated to leave that room, too. Did you sense it? That intimation of some future moment when everyone will be assembled, ready to have their flimsy alibis and petty grudges dragged into the light. Damn, I love it. Even the seemingly innocent are forced to admit they have harbored dark motives, have hidden terrible longings."

A fierce wistfulness had come into Zapf's face. "And finally—" He threw up his arms. "—from amidst the chaos that violence engenders, a redeemer appears, capable of sorting the sheep from the goats. One genuinely guilty soul gets fingered and puts on the badge of shame—for the group knows he's bound for perdition. And the <u>order of creation is restored</u>."

Through the hedge, we found Culligan's room in the cottage. There was a bed, a table, a dresser, and a pile of newspapers. The guy was a reader. Zapf went through the dresser while I pulled a battered canvas suitcase out from under the bed. It was full of workman's clothing. I discovered an envelope folded inside a faded shirt. I scanned the handwritten letter.

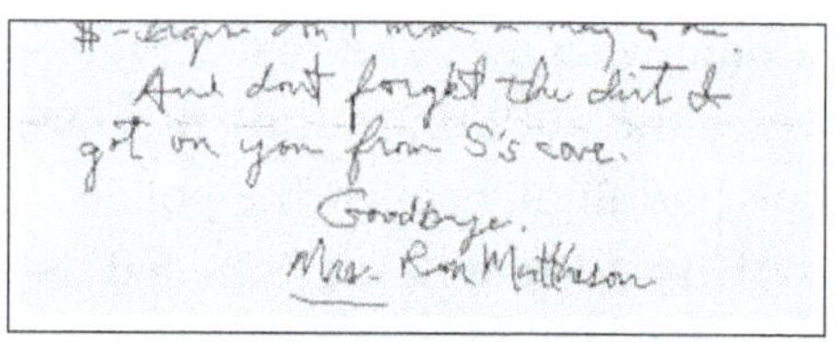

The Letter

"This looks like a lead," I told Zapf.

He examined the letter. "Good work,

son," he said, squinting as if he wished he had a <u>magnifying glass</u>.

Actually he didn't look that old—maybe about my age. "Why," I asked, "is your name familiar to me?

"Oh, you probably seen one of my advertisements."

The Editor's Column Part III

In the dead man's cottage, Zapf studied the postmark on the letter. Then he put everything back in the suitcase and slid it under the bed. "Come on," he said. "We'd better get back to the house.

Passing through the garden, I reminded Zapf that I'd picked up the sound of a car.

"What sort of vehicle do you reckon it was?"

"Sounded like a compact," I said. "Probably an older Japanese import—four cylinders. Missing a little, as I recall—and burning oil. I'd guess a fouled spark-plug and a sticky valve. Drive it over sixty for half an hour— you'd blow the engine."

Zapf was staring at me, as if I were the crazy one. "Makes sense," he finally said. "A professional hit man would drive a throw-away.

"So, Sable's wife didn't shoot Culligan."

"Nah. But she seen something bad happen." Zapf looked at the house. "Hey, kid. You go in there. I gotta catch up with that car. Tell Sable I'm on the case. I'll send you a report!" Already Zapf was sprinting across the lawn.

The philosopher-detective sped off in an old orange Datsun sedan.

In Caxton's house, a couple over-weight guys in white had wrapped the body in a plastic sheet. They were heaving it onto a stretcher. A white-haired police photographer was packing up his gear.

"You Strether?" demanded a slender guy in a suit. His face looked the way I now felt: sallow and exhausted. He introduced himself as Detective Sgt. Trask and consulted a list of names. "You were out on the deck with the others," he said.

"Yes."

"And we can reach you here?"

"Yes."

"Okay. We'll be in touch."

"Fine." I didn't volunteer anything I knew about the dead man.

Sable was slumped on the couch. One of the cushions—the blood-stained one—was missing.

I sat down in an armchair and asked where Bill Caxton was.

"Off to the airport," said Sable. "Loren's a wreck. But they believe she's telling the truth about a stranger barging in to shoot Peter."

Ah, I decided. The hit man.

Sgt. Trask was watching us. He took a seat on the coffee table and faced Sable. "The victim was your houseman, right? Did you know he had a criminal record? He's got prison tattoos on his left knuckles."

"Goodness," said Sable and looked at the floor. "I hired him on the coast to look after my summer place. The last few weeks we had him doing odd jobs at my house next door. You don't think Peter was involved with criminals?"

The sergeant sighed as if he were dealing with a moron.

"Of course," Sable said, "he was a drifter, a loner. He hardly left the house. But he was a good worker—in the yard."

"Maybe he was hiding out at your place," said Trask.

Sable looked baffled. "But—these two houses are always full of people. It's an odd choice for a hide-out."

Trask asked if he could talk to Mrs. Sable again.

"She'd better rest," said Sable. "Our doctor gave her a sedative.

From the next room I heard a woman moaning in a shrill minor key. It hurt my ears.

Two days later I heard from Zapf. He

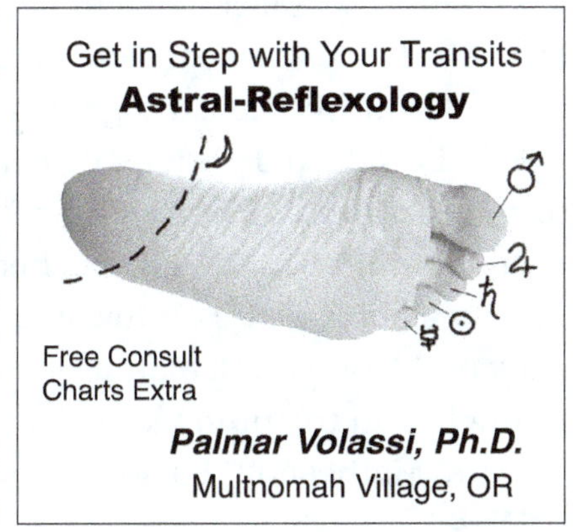

He preferred to keep in touch by U.S. Mail. I learned that he didn't carry a cell-phone. His pockets jingled with the quarters he plugged into pay-phones. He claimed to know a few places around the state that still had old-fashioned phone booths—the kind with a seat and a ceiling-light fan that went on when you pulled the folding door closed.

I've kept the little reports Zapf has sent so far. I reprint them below:

Zapf's Report #1

Day 1

I drove west out of the wooded West Hills. A thin cloud of burned engine oil still hung over the roadway. I lost it at Highway 26, the route to the Oregon Coast.

It didn't make sense. I'd expected the trail to go straight to the PDX airport—or maybe east across the high desert to Reno or Vegas. Then I remembered the postmark on the dead man's letter: Manzanita, a little town on the coast.

The woman who signed the letter, Mrs. Ron Matheson, had told Culligan she didn't want him back in her life. What had passed between them, years ago, was over. "Goodbye," she'd signed it—with a period. But she'd also added a curious threat: "And don't forget the dirt I got on you—from S's Cove."

Ninety minutes later I reached Cannon Beach. The place was crowded with tourists. I found a local phone book and found an R. Matheson still living in Manzanita. I punched in the number. A woman answered.

"Mrs. Matheson?" I said.

"Yes?"

"My name is Zapf. Maybe you've seen my TV commercials?"

"I don't think so."

"Well—I'm calling about Peter Culligan ."

"What about him?"

"He's dead."

There was a silence. "Serves him right," she said.

"I'm on the case. Maybe you have some information."

"I haven't seen him in thirty years."

When I insisted on seeing her, she said she didn't want any detective coming to her house, to her neighborhood. But she could drive up to Cannon Beach, right away.

I waited half an hour on the steps in front of <u>the ice cream store</u>. The steps were stained with vanilla, mint, and chocolate chip cookie dough.

When Mrs. Matheson arrived, I faced an overweight woman in her sixties. She wore shorts and a dark shirt and sunglasses. Her breasts sagged and her legs were mottled with blue veins. But I had a hunch that years ago she'd had curves like the hull of a racing yacht. If I'd met her then, she'd have been gorgeous—as usual, out of my league. So, eyeing her now, I felt—you could say—oddly attracted to her.

On the beach we found a big driftwood <u>log to sit on</u>. Gulls hung in the air overhead, kids flew kites, and the mild roar of the Pacific surf sounded in the distance.

"So," she sighed. "Pete is dead.

I gave her the story of the shooting, and finding her letter.

She looked at me through her dark sunglasses. "Who did it?" she asked, her voice encrusted with memories.

"You tell me."

"You're not with the police?"

"I'm a private investigator."

"Listen, I haven't seen him for thirty years. I've got a nice family, a good husband. But I heard from him about six months ago—from Reno. He claimed he was in for a big pay-off. He wanted to see me." She looked down the beach as if searching the past. "Peter always had big plans," she said. "What a dumb chump he was."

"How did you get mixed up with him?"

"Oh, I was a nurse's aid in a Portland hospital—that was in 1958. I was just out of high school. He came in all beat up from a fight on the docks. But he was a charming guy. I didn't learn until later he'd been in the state prison."

"That pay-off in Reno. Was it gambling he was counting on?"

"I don't know what it was."

"Do you have his letter?"

"I tore it up."

"So forty years, ago you were married. Then you were divorced?"

"Not exactly." She looked down at her feet. "Listen, I've got a new life now."

"You said in your letter that he should remember S. Cove. What hap-

pened there?"

Her face went blank. "I don't know what you're talking about."

"There's a place called *Smuggler's Cove* just down the coast," I said.

"There is?" She made a grim face.

"It's part of a State Park now. Some maps call it *Sand Beach*. Was Peter Culligan a smuggler? Drugs, guns, Mexicans, exotic animals?"

"*Smuggler's?*" she said. "That name comes from the 1920s—Prohibition."

"But something happened there—probably in 1958?"

"It was so long ago," she said. "Someone hired me as a nurse. A guy with a pregnant woman. That's all I remember."

I wondered if Mrs. Matheson was the pregnant women herself. "What was this guy's name?"

She gripped her purse and sat up. I was losing her.

"Hey," I said. "There was a murder today. The police will find that letter."

"Murder? How would I know anything about it."

"And another thing," I said. "The hitman was headed in this direction. He wouldn't be after you, would he?"

There was fear in her face, but she wrestled it down into blankness. "I don't think so," she said. Then she stood and walked up the sand back to town.

I sat on the log and listened to the gulls crying overhead. A kid walked by carrying a kite that had crashed and broken.

Sable and Caxton had hired me to find a missing heir. But there was something half-hearted about their search. When I'd asked about where this missing son had been conceived,

Caxton had mentioned the coast—but he hadn't mentioned a birthdate. The boy, according to Sable, must be in his mid-forties by now. Now this shooting had brought me to Cannon Beach. Was it possible that Mrs. Matheson, in 1958, had been the woman who bore Caxton's son?

I walked back to my car and drove south. On the way to Manzanita I passed *Oswald West State Park*. Highway 101 cuts around the coast-end of Neahkahnie Mountain and then descends the south slope to sea level. On the way, <u>there's a nice view</u> of Manzanita. Driving in from 101, you can tell it's a nice town: a couple restaurants, a tavern, a grocery, a handful of motels. The main street ends at the ocean. Gov. Oswald West, back in 1913, was the one who declared Oregon's coast a public highway. You can walk the sand and rocks from the California border all the way to the Columbia River and not hit a property line.

Inside the grocery, I spotted a young woman with an infant seat propped in her grocery cart.

"Excuse me?" I said. "I'm trying to find an obstetrician in town. Can you recommend one?"

"Oh," she said. "We go to the clinic in Wheeler. Sometimes the hospital in Tillamook."

"I see. There's not one in Manzanita."

"Well, there's Doc. Milburn Stone. But he's been retired for years."

"An older man?"

"Past eighty, I'd say."

"Do you know where he lives?

"Everyone knows the Stone house. It's right on the upper coast road."

I drove north from town. The house was hard to miss—a two-story Victorian right on the road with a nice view off the back porch. When I knocked on the front door I heard shuffling footsteps inside. A pair of grizzled eyes peered out when the door opened a crack.

"Doctor Milburn Stone?"

"I don't practice anymore."

"My name's Zapf. I'm a private eye. Maybe you've seen my commercials."

He opened the door wider and squinted at me. "You look like that fellow who guides the Big-Foot tours."

"That's me, too."

"Okay, come in," he said. Doc Stone was a formerly big man who'd lost a foot in height from walking stooped over—as if he'd spent the last twenty years carrying a burden on his back. You meet a lot of characters in my line of work. Right away, I knew Doc here was a real man of the West.

I stepped inside, following his sweet bent shuffle, though a parlor and into an elaborate office. The place gave me an odd feeling.

Milburn Stone, M.D.
—circa 1958

The place was set up like Freud's study: oriental rugs on the couches, Egyptian figurines on every flat surface. Stone indicated a chair for me and eased himself down behind a desk. A foot-high statue of Osiris blocked our view face to face. He shoved it aside.

"Now, about Bigfoot—" he said. "I prefer the Native American name: *Sasquatch.*"

"Me too," I said. Actually, it's the name of a tribe—a lost tribe—known only by rumor."

"Yup," he said. "The Sasquatch. A mysterious population which genuine Indians regarded as brutish and hairy. They may have occupied this coastal area since the last ice age. Nobody knows where they came from."

"You've done some research," I said.

"It's a hobby. Like my little obsession with the constellation Orion."

"Ah," I said. "Orion's belt—and the pyramids."

"Touché. I see we share some interests in common. But there's a difference between us. You've commercialized this Sasquatch legend."

"Not at all," I said. "My Big Foot tours explore the Mt. Hood National Forest, with side-trips along the Columbia

River gorge. My clients seem equally interested in D. B. Cooper."

Doc Stone's eyes crinkled into a grin, and he chuckled from his belly. We had a good laugh together.

When he'd caught his breath, he finally said, "So you're here on other business."

"Does your memory go back to 1958?"

"It was the height of my practice."

"There was a birth that year—and a woman from this area was hired to help the young mother."

"I recall the event precisely," said Stone. But I forgot that woman they hired. Callahan? Kerrigan. Was that her name?"

"Culligan?"

"That's it. A Mrs. Culligan and her hulking husband."

"Your memory of the distant past is petty good," I said.

"Actually I had refresher course a couple months ago. Another inquiry like your own."

"In this office?"

He sat in that very chair. A fellow about your size, but better dressed. He wore a blue blazer, had his long hair pulled back tight—and wore sunglasses."

"Wynk de Worde."

"He called himself *Caxton*. Said he was trying to find out about his mother."

"And you believed him?"

"He seemed like a nice fellow."

"Well, I've met him," I said, feeling indignant. "He's an operator, a phony. How did he locate you?"

"He'd somehow ordered a copy of a birth certificate— the Oregon State version. My name is on it."

"You have copies here?"

Doc Stone levered himself out of his chair and made his way to a dented green filing cabinet. From a manila folder he drew out a page and brought it over. "This is the version I filled out," he said.

The <u>faded document</u> told me that *Wah-wah-taysee Caxton* was born at 4:15 p.m. April 18, 1958 to *Winona <u>   ?   </u>*. The <u>last name</u> was hard to make out. The form listed <u>the father</u> as *William Caxton*.

Doc Stone was looking at me with crinkled eyes. "Is that what you're after?" he said.

Damn those fools, Caxton and Sable, I thought. They could have given me this information at the beginning. For one thing, the birthdate surprised me. And de Worde's gall: elbowing his way into the Caxton family. Of course, in my line of work you get hit with a lot of surprises.

"What was the mother like?" I asked.

Doc Stone took the document and studied it. "She was a lovely slender woman—and very pregnant when I first saw her. The California fellow she listed as the father only showed up once. He paid me in advance. She was living in a shanty—actually an ingenious sort of hut—in the woods on the other side of the mountain."

"Neahkahnie Mountain?"

"You're not a treasure-hunter, too?" chuckled Stone.

"I know the stories. Now, about this hut—"

"I only went down there twice. Once for the actual birthing. It was quite a difficult and extended affair. The girl's mother was there: she was a strange creature who spoke a very distinct but foreign tongue. I hiked down the next evening at sunset. The old woman did a kind of christening ceremony. After that they had help from that Culligan woman whom Caxton hired." But it was a gorgeous setting. A nice view of the cove."

"Smuggler's Cove," I said.

"These days the surfers have discovered it. Of course, it wasn't a state park then. Only local people went down there—and Indians."

"Was this blond woman an Indian?"

"It was hard to tell. I recall her lovely mouth, long glossy hair down her back—and her eyes: such a pale green. Such thick lashes. An other-worldly look. It took you in deep, that look..." Doc Stone was lost in a dream.

"She made quite an impression on you," I said.

Doc looked up at me. "I've never forgotten her," he said. "Of course, I was a younger man then."

"If she was still alive—"

"She'd be in her sixties," he said.

"Do you know what happened to her?"

"There was some trouble—after she gave birth. A friend of Culligan's showed up on a motorcycle. I'd seen the two of them around town. Then they all took off somewhere."

"That's all you know?"

"Isn't that enough?

I sensed that Doc Stone was holding something back. Everybody holds something back. But I didn't want to push him too hard. I got up, tipped my hat and said, "I reckon I'll be headin' out. Thanks, and—so long."

Zapf's Report #2
Day 2

I mailed my first report back to Strether in Portland. Then I spent the night in the back seat of my Datsun. After breakfast I drove over to the State Police substation in Nehalem. I knew the Sheriff there, Jack Cooper.

"What's it this time?" he said, looking up from his desk. "More Big-foot sightings?" It's an old joke between us. Cooper is a lanky gray-haired man past retirement age.

"Does your memory go back to 1958?" I asked.

"Matter of fact, I was a rookie then. A cadet from the Police Academy. Learning the ropes."

"Do you remember some trouble with an Indian woman and a couple rough-necks—one of them named Culligan?"

"Was Doc Stone involved?"

"Probably."

"There was a case—one of my first—where Doc turned in a Missing Persons report. An Indian woman who'd just given birth. I remember because it involved an escapee from the State Prison."

"Not Culligan?"

"Nah, this was—now lemme think. *Shoulders Nelson.* He fit the description that Doc gave us. There was another fellow with him. Could have been your Culligan."

"What about the MPR?"

"Doc thought the woman had been kidnapped. Disappeared, anyway."

"And an infant—newborn?"

"It's coming back to me now. I was ordered to drive up there—north of Manzanita, overlooking the cove—to take a look. I found the charred timbers and foundation stones of what must have been a big shack. The embers were still smoking when I got there. In the bushes were some dirty diapers. And the track of a motorcycle—with a sidecar."

"Shoulders Nelson," I said. "He rode a motorcycle."

"That's right. We put out an APB. But I don't think anything ever came of it. Maybe I can find the report. There are old files in the basement."

"I'd appreciate it," I said and headed out the door. I'd decided to pay a visit to Mrs. Matheson.

Her address in Manzanita led me to a modest coast-style bungalow with weathered cedar siding. A kid's skate-board

lay discarded in the grass.

When she answered the door and saw it was me, her face grew taut and hard. "I told you I didn't want you to come here," she said. Then she checked to see if any neighbors were in sight. "You better step inside," she said.

I followed her through a cluttered living room and out a patio door into the back yard.

"You didn't mention a jailbird called Shoulders Nelson," I said, figuring the name would make her flinch.

She had her arms crossed defensively. One hand was tucked in—so you couldn't see it. Were the fingers curled, or spread flat against her ribs? Or did she grip a small caliber pistol?

"Never heard of him," she finally said.

"The State Police have an old kidnapping case still open. They'd be interested to learn that you were part of it."

"It wasn't a kidnapping!" she cried. Then her mouth clamped shut and she clasped her hands together as if in prayer.

"Maybe we better sit down," I said, indicating a lawn chair.

It was <u>a nice little yard</u>. Birds made a racket in the trees.

Over the next ten minutes I learned that Shoulders had been a ladies' man. He'd spent some time in California with Neal Cassidy. Even the pregnant woman— her name was *Winona*—seemed charmed by him. But Shoulders had a mean streak that kept everybody in line, especially his buddy Culligan.

After the birthing was over, the old crone—Winona's mother—took off for Neahkahnie Mountain. When she didn't come back, it didn't seem to surprise anyone. Culligan had an old '49 Ford parked up on the highway. Shoulders had his motorcycle and side-car. Winona had a big wad of bills. So they all took off. Their destination was Montana, but somewhere in the middle of Washington state, Shoulders changed his mind and headed west. Mrs. Matheson and Culligan tried to keep up in the Ford. Outside Tacoma they lost sight of the motorcycle. For them it was the end of the road-trip. Because Tacoma looked like a nice place to settle down—that's just what they did. Their marriage lasted two years.

When she'd finished, I sat and listened to <u>the birds overhead</u>.

"Please," she said. "I have a decent life here—grandchildren, even. Don't stir up the past."

"Then why," I asked, "did you hire a gun to kill your ex: Peter Culligan? Precisely because he was threatening to bring up the past?"

She looked stunned. "You think I could do that?"

I glanced around at the nice yard, at the grandchildren's toys in the sandbox. "You had a lot to lose," I said.

Her eyes were smeared with the dirt I'd dredged up. Just then a patch of sun drifted over her garden. I remembered my first reaction seeing her: she'd been a gorgeous dame.

"Okay," I said. "I'll keep you out of the case. And the information you've given me—I'll keep that for my confidential use."

"Is there a price?" she asked.

"There's no price," I said. "Just keep your nose clean, kiddo."

Out front where I'd parked my Datsun something funny was going on. The driver's side door was open. Some jerk had his head under my steering wheel, trying to hot-wire my car.

He must have heard me coming, because he slid out fast and started up the street. Then he stopped to look back. He was a greasy little weasel with a knife in one hand.

But he'd picked the wrong guy's car. I'm a black-belt in TaeKwon Do.

I sprinted straight at him and gave him a Flying Side Piercing Kick (*Twimyo Yop Cha Busigi*). He went down but staggered up. I hit him again with a Knifehand Reverse High Front Strike (*Gunnun So Sonkal Dung Sonkal Bandae Nopunde Ap Tae-rigi*), spun to deliver a High Turning Kick (*Nopunde Dollyo Chagi*), then added a Middle Back Piercing Kick (*Kaunde Dwi Cha Jirugi*). Finally I stepped in and gripped him in a good old *Bear Hug*. He wheezed and

The Korean owner of a convenience store taught Zapf the secrets of Tae-Kwon Do.

Above: **ON A DANGEROUS STREET** Zapf delivers his version of the deadly *Twimyo Yop Cha Busigi.*

choked. I squeezed harder. Finally he cried, "I give!" and I let him slump to the ground.

That's when I noticed the car parked up the street—an older Japanese import. The motor was running, probably for a quick get-away. Black smoke sputtered out of the tailpipe. It had to be the car Strether heard after the shooting.

I grabbed the greasy guy's ear and pulled him to his feet. "Who sent you to knock off Peter Culligan?" I demanded. "The lady who lives here?"

"J7ꝺ Ѡ[," he said.

"Oh, a wise-guy, huh?" I twisted his ear-lobe.

"ᘯ! Who the J7ꝺ are you?"

I put a thumb in his nostril and gave his face a good shaking.

"Okay! Okay!" he hollered.

"What's your name?

"Ow! Okay! It's Tommy. Tommy Lemberg."

"How much did she pay you?"

"She's just Pete's old lady. I ain't even seen her yet."

"Seen her for what?"

"To say hello from— Wait a J7ꝺ1ℛ minute. Pete got shot?"

"You ought to know, Tommy. You were the trigger-man."

"ᘯ, I was outta that house when I heard a shot. I beat it."

"What were you doing there?"

"I was supposed to rough somebody up. But Culligan answered the door. We're old buddies. We both worked for Schwartz in Reno. Pete was a little suspicious of me showing up. But said he was real glad to see me, and I would do him this favor—locate his old wife?

[continued on p. 106]

Innocent girl taken for ride

**#2 Searching
for Margo**

[continued from p. 51]

Serial fiction by Anton Garamond

*The story so far: Luke Waxman—newcomer to the
west—has driven all night in a rented truck. He's
hurrying to deliver a ring to someone in Portland
named Margo.*

L uke hallucinated a far-off, white mountain as he
gripped the wheel and hollered all the way down to
the bridge over the Columbia. Behind him he heard glass-
ware shattering, furniture busting up. Then the brakes
caught, and he was down safe.

On the Oregon side, things looked different. In Hood
River, for example, he asked a sail-boarder for directions
to "Jubitz," the only address Olga had given him. The fellow abruptly sprang into the air, spun about, and landed
facing the wind. "Follow any big truck. But you're crazy to
go to Portland."

Luke ignored the warning and tailed a convoy through
the Gorge. Sure enough, north of Portland they pulled in
at a big sign: JUBITZ. The place was jammed with big
Freightliner and Peterbilt rigs.

Inside, a guy with a bullhorn was giving truckers line-
dance lessons. Big men in jeans, leather jackets, and
cowboy hats linked arms and stamped their boots forward, then back, to the left—kick.

At the counter, a waitress told Luke that Margo had
quit. "She got a job at some kind of university. *Vanport.*
Me, I wouldn't risk working in Portland."

"Thanks," he said and went to check the phone books.

Oddly, nothing called "Vanport" was listed. And why did people think Portland was hazardous?

Outside he examined the ring he was supposed to deliver. What had Olga called it? A Hag's Ring.

"Nice ring," said a young woman in a trench coat. She was petite—short hair spiked in a punk mess that he found endearing. At her belly, she cradled an enor-mous ripe bulge. Her ears and nose were free of piercings. He'd grown accustomed to eyebrow rings, nostril pearls, and tongue studs among the college women he taught.

"Gosh, your baby must be due soon," he said."

"I guess," she replied vaguely. "I been waiting here three hours. My boyfriend said he'd meet me. This has gotta be the wrong place. I need help."

To Luke, a pleaser, *help* was the magic word. When he offered her a ride, she treated him to that old smile.

He carried her satchel to his yellow Riter truck, where he had to lift her in.

Once they were rolling, he said, "You probably don't want to go to Portland, right?"

She'd put her feet up on the dashboard. "Take a left here," she said.

"Say, your name isn't 'Margo' is it?"

"'Monica,'" she said. "Hey, I feel weird. Like, there are these pains?"

"Oh?" he said.

"Yeah. They've been coming and going."

"You're joking, of course."

"Oh!" she wailed suddenly. There was a commotion at the belly of her trench coat. "Oh, help!"

Luke swerved the truck over to the curb

"It's coming out!" she shrieked.

"Hold on!" yelled Luke. "Hold on!"

[continued

Big baby poops out in truck

**#3 Searching
for Margo**

Serial fiction by Anton Garamond

*The story so far: Luke has driven from Minnesota to
locate someone named Margo. But now he's offered
a ride to a young woman. Abruptly she's gone into
labor!*

Monica gripped her belly and yelled. Luke stopped and
leapt out. This north Portland warehouse district
looked deserted. He raced to the passenger door and flung
it open.

Beneath her trench coat, between her legs, it looked
like— A little hairy head!

Heart racing, he watched a little face appear. And arms!
He gripped the fingers and felt them seize his thumbs.

"Oh!" shrieked Monica as Luke yanked.

"Wah!" hollered the infant.

"Jeez," gasped Luke. "It's wearing a diaper!"

"It's a miracle!" she cried.

"It's got teeth!" he yelled.

"You're kidding," she said.

Instinctively he drew the infant against his chest. Out
the back of its diaper oozed warm baby poop. Crouched
there in the door of a rented truck and holding a stinky
baby that looked at least six months old, Luke cursed his
luck.

Monica was fishing in her satchel. The trench coat had
fallen open. Goodness, what was she wearing—nothing? He
caught a glimpse of legs, bare all the way to the thigh. She
was holding out a plastic bottle with a nipple.

"Here," she said. "Give him some of this stuff."

"That was a dumb trick," said Luke.

"I needed a ride. Women with kids don't get rides."

"But—" He held out messy hands.

"Can't you just, sort of—push it back in?"

"Jeez. Hand me those paper towels."

Luke carried the baby around to the driver's seat.

"Gak-a gurk," it squealed.

Luke wiped away poop to reveal a penis and a bad case of diaper rash. The kid broke into a wail. Tears welled out of his eyes and ran down to his ears.

"Hush," Luke whispered. "Hush."

Monica handed him another diaper. "Make it good and tight," she said. "It's the only one I got."

"It figures," he said. "Do you have some cream for this rash?"

"What rash?"

Suddenly a hand forced Luke's head down hard against the steering wheel! Someone yanked the key out of the ig-nition.

"Okay, let him up, Garbage," said a voice.

Luke spun around. He found himself looking into a big toothless grin.

The guy was Hell's Angels type—bare-chested in a jean-jacket with the sleeves cut off, shaggy beard, head balding.

The other one—a wiry guy wearing a knit cap—tossed the key in the air.

The big one caught it in a massive fist. "Hey, I guess we got ourselves a truck."

[continued on page 101]

Longfellow's Sasquatch

Arthur Strether
sheds new light on the
origins of Hiawatha

Before even glancing at the next page,
please take the Pop Quiz on p. 233.

Poking through the archives of the Longfellow Research Library in Minneapolis, I ran across a faded brown folder stuffed with old letters. Written in the fall

Longfellow Library
on Minnehaha Parkway—Minneapolis

of 1854, they were signed "Henry Wadsworth Longfellow, Cambridge, Massachusetts," and addressed to Henry Rowe Schoolcraft, the Indian Agent and ethnologist.

Longfellow was at work on his epic, *Song of Hiawatha*, and writes to thank Schoolcraft for certain clarifications he's received: about the location of a precipice of red pipestone rock, about the enigmatic death of Winona (daughter of Nokomis and Hiawatha's mother), and about the practice of greasing birch-bark canoes with the oil of *Mishe-Nahma*.[1] Then he

Schoolcraft

---

[1] See *Moby Dick*, Chapter LXXXIV, (Pitchpoling): "Queequeg believed strongly in anointing his boat..." with whale oil.

appends this curious apology:

I am grateful for the glossary of terms your wife Jane prepared, written out in their curious—if I may so call it—script. Especially the following items: Wah-wah-taysee: ·/ʂ/ʂρʈſʜ, Chibiabos: ·ʒ|ʜʂ|oſ, Megissogwon: ·ʌʅριſʅρ/ʌʅ, and pau-puk-keewis: ·kʃʍɕʜ/ıſ, for these match the measure I've hit upon for my poem. But I have been informed that there is no way to reproduce such characters on the printed page for publication. Moreover, my correspondent, Freiligrath, tells me that these symbols Jane has so artfully mastered are clearly derived from an Old Norse runic alphabet. Is it possible that your wife was mistaken when she claimed that this "Indian script" and the legend "were brought across the continent" by her ancestors from the Kingdom of Mudje-keewis, the Portal of the Sunset?

Out from another envelope tumbled a manuscript and a letter that Jane Schoolcraft[2] had sent Longfellow. Perhaps he intended to return them to her. I reproduce both below:

Dear Mr. Longfellow,

The northwestern <u>Sasquatch</u> Tribe, from whom this legend is derived, no longer exists. But copies of their story, written out in a script they claim to have invented, were brought across the continent by my ancestors. Believing that it may provoke your curiosity, I enclose a translation. But I have employed their phonetic symbols to render my English. translation. I am confident that a writer of your eminence

------

[2] <u>Jane's</u> story-telling parents were Chippewa and Norwegian, and her husband never seems to have acknowledged his debt to her skills as a translator. He makes no use of her special interest in the role women played in Native American culture—for example, the dominance of clan mothers within the Iroquois Confederacy. And nowhere does he mention the legend this astonishing manuscript records.

will find it amusing to decode the legend.

Sincerely,   Jane (Mrs. Henry Rowe Schoolcraft)

ǫ7S iᔆ /7ʔ ǫ⅃1 ·ḋ/ʜᔿ ·ᔿoḋoᔿiS
thus it was that Queen Nokomis

Key to Sasquatch Phonetic Alphabet

ρ	as in	**th**us	/	as in	**w**oe
7	as in	**u**s	ʔ	as in	**z**oo
l	as in	**i**t	ɹ	as in	**a**t
1	as in	**t**ot	ḋ	as in	**K**ick
O	as in	**oa**k	ʃ	as in	**m**om
S	as in	**s**o	ι	as in	**i**n / **n**o
ʜ	as in	**s**ee			

/ᴜ1 Jᴅᴆ Jᴅɪᴦ ɣᴖ ᴐᴐᴄ ᴄᴧᵹɣᴄS

ι	as in	**b**et	ᴐ	as in	**r**oar
J	as in	**f**ee	ᴧ	as in	**o**n
ᴆ	as in	**o**r	ɣ	as in	**h**a
ᴆ	as in	**th**igh	∩	as in	**er**
ᵧ	as in	**oi**l	ᴧ	as in	**ou**t
ᴄ	as in	**l**oll	O	as in	**oa**k
ᵹ	as in	hu**ng**	ᴧ	as in	**ou**t

[Also find a key to the Phonetic Alphabet on p. 235].

So, decoding phonetic symbols is not your cup of tea?

A Special Offer for Subscribers to *The American Quarterly Review!*

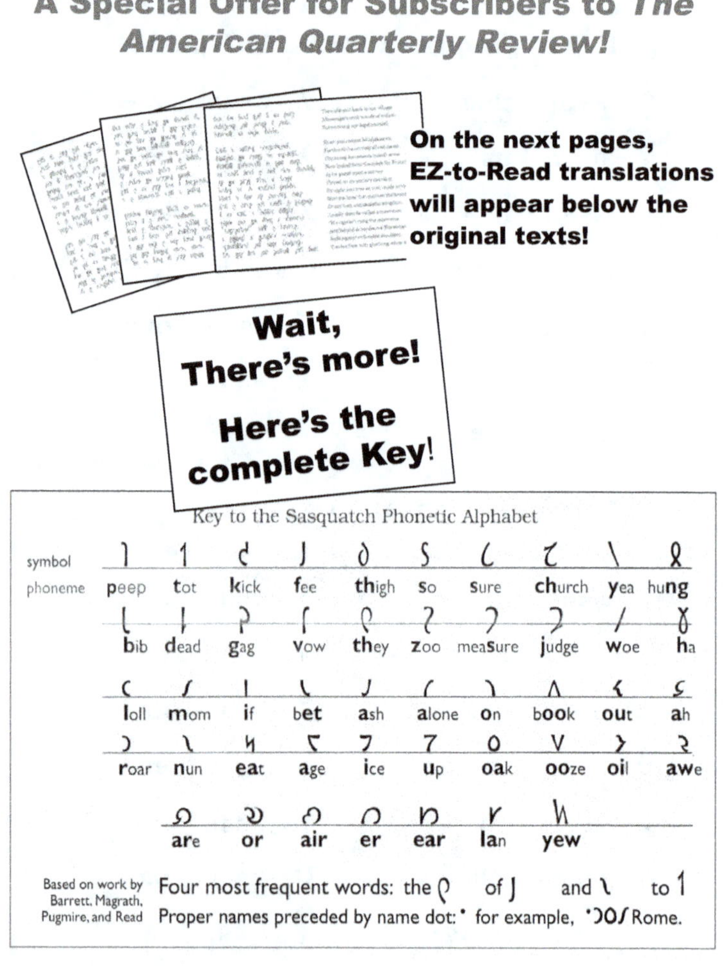

Thus it was that Queen Nokomis
Went forth from her royal longhouse
And descended to the water,
Where the strangers were assembled.
Bearded were they, and wore armor
Polished smooth like dark obsidian.
On their faces they wore looks of
Wonder at our warriors, also bearded,
And the flowers streaming from the
Raven tresses of our ruler.

One there was they called <u>Sir Francis</u>,
Such a proud and haughty fellow
That to keep from laughing outright
We bit our tongues and pinched our noses,
For he held aloft a pinion,
Waved it grandly, gestured madly,
At the landscape northward, southward

Then into the sand he thrust it,
One hand pointing to his bosom.
All this time he hollered at us
In his silly sing-song language.
When he ceased he seemed annoyed at
Birds that sung among the thickets,
As if silence better matched
The answer he imagined hearing.
But the air was full of fragrance,
And the streamlets laughed and glis-
tened.

Blithely forward stepped our ruler,
Daughter of the moon, Nokomis,
Faced the stranger, and bestowed the
Sort of smile that conquers nations.
To his knees the knave sunk humbled,
Bowed his forehead lower, lower,
'Till in sand it was embedded.

ou Ch Su1 pd 1 co pici]
rcSi2o? /io /si2 J /ico,
S7rrui8 co cnpc dciSc,

Lo1 i 2o17u ·rn2rdu/uS.
Joo/io zu ro7pi rc ou-JcS1,
dc7zi8 pdvrui5 ii [oo or?.
ic cnd1 Jcu1 p rud ·So ·Jorisis,
J? zu pczi 7lu s Sorc
lciri ii ji cizri pnSdi.
S1oc1 i 1ov J? /uc-rci ooo?
Li1 p cziz pu1 rod1 p [ci pu?
J co c7L i luSJrc di8irr.
cuicu pu zu dzci s dovrri:
"u[rpcio!" o78 p S7rri?.
i [iyoci! s zuiuSri ·io Srri,
·[7cci81ri! /io roic Locio?,
1ui zi? JcS /io pcisui8 /71 1uo!

Then she sent back to our village
Messengers with wands of willow,
Summoning our legal counsel,

Short and rotund Mudjekeewis.
Forthwith he arrived all red-faced,
Clutching documents in both arms.
Now looked faint the meek Sir Francis,
As he gazed upon a survey
Plotted on an ancient deerskin.
Straight and true as well-made arrows
Shot the lines that marked the bound-
aries
Of our lush and peaceful kingdom.
Loudly then he called a crewman:
"Navigator!" rung the summons.
And behold! A handsome Norseman,
Bulkington! with noble shoulders,
Tan his face with glist'ning white teeth!

ɔɔʏ ıʋ cɕ J ʃʋl ʋ ɕ7ʃlʀS,
[ʋʋ1 ʋ ʋʔ ʂ Sɕʂcɔ S17ʃʋ
S1ɔɕʋʔ ʋolɕɕʌʔ, cɔʋʔ ʋ ɕʋpcʔ.
Jıℛɔ ʋ ʂ S7ʋ, ɣʋ ʃ7lɔʃ,
"1ʋʃlʀc J ρ Sʋ1ıℛ S7ʋ"?
ʔc ρıS 17ʃ ɕɔ ɕ/ʋʋ ·ʋɕoʃıS
ɣʃʃ ʃɕʋ1ɕʋ ʂ ɣʔ1ʋ S7cʋS.
ʋɕ ɕʋ Sloɕ, "ʋ ɔʋʃ ɕɔ ccℛpıʔ?"
"\ʂ," ɣʋ Sʋ, "7 Sʋ S7ʃ ɾɔʃʔ ʋ1
cʌɕ Jʀʃıc\ɔ, cɔɕ ʃʂ ɔvʋʔ 7J
·oɕ ·7Scʌʃıɕ ʋʃ1 ı'J S17ʃʋ."
71ɔʃ ʋ ɣıʔ ·ʋɕSʃʋʔ ʃɕSʋ1,
Sɕʋʔ cɔɕ ρʋʔ ɕʋ ɕʋʃɔʋɣʋʋʃʋ,
ɕ lɔɣʋlS ɣʋJ-ρʋS1 ρɔ ʃʋʋıℛ.
"cʃʋ J 7S," ɕʋ cʋJ1 ʋʋc71ʃ.
ρ7S ɕʋ ɕɕʃ 1 1ʋc ρıS S1ɕʋ:
"ʋ ρ ·oɕ ·17ʃ, cʋʔʃʋ 1ʋcʔ 7S,
ɕʔıʔ ʋʋɔ ρ ʟıʔʋʋıℛ,

Trained in lore of map and compass,
Bent and as a scholar studied
Strange notations, lines and angles.
Finger on a sign, he muttered,
"1ʋʃlʀc J ρ Sʋ1ıℛ S7ʋ"?
All this time our queen Nokomis
Had maintained a haughty silence.
Now she spoke, "You read our language?"
"Ja," he said, "I see some vords dat
Look familiar, like da runes uff
Old Icelandic dat I'fe studied."
Uttered in his Norseman's accent,
Sounds like these she comprehended,
Or perhaps half-guessed their meaning.
"Land of Ice," she laughed delighted.
Thus she came to tell this story:
"In the Old Time, legend tells us,
Ages nearer the beginning

When the heavens were closer to us
And the Gods were more familiar,
Our ancestors made a journey
Westward from an ice-bound nation.
First in boats and then on sledges,
Hunting huge beasts with their lances,
While the greener vistas beckoned
To the portals of the sunset,
To the earth's remotest borders.
Here in this cove, at this ocean,
Their long trek at last they ended.
On the mountain here behind me
Sacred <u>Neahkahnie</u> Mountain,
They erected in a circle
Timbers spaced in such a manner
They predicted sunrise, moonset.
Further eastward they had fashioned
Such a temple by a river,

And the two now marked the mid-line
Of the empire they had conquered.
New arrivals, dark marauders,
From the north now swept down fiercely.
But perplexed, they dropped their weapons
When our women warriors faced them.
And they cocked their heads like pet dogs
Trying to decipher drawings,
Surveys proving that the owners
Of the land now stood before them.
For the notion that a people
Would inscribe upon the landscape
Lines of ownership unswerving
Was a strange and alien concept.
Thus we granted them safe passage
To the south, like all the others
Who attempted an invasion.
Thousands like them over centuries

Made the detour 'round our borders.
Now the land is full to bursting;
Many peoples press against us.
But the noblest of their warriors, though
they pluck their beards with clamshells,
Generous dowries have presented
To the mothers of our daughters;
So we welcome them among us.
Thus a long and peaceful history,
In our ancient written language,
Was recorded as we lived it.
Queens there were, each named Nokomis
And each bore a lovely daughter
Named Winona 'til the time came,
At her mother's fated passing,
To assume the title, Ruler."
With these words, Nokomis faltered
With both hands her face she covered,

As if in a swoon she stood there.

All exasperated paced the
English captain, rude Sir Francis.
"What in Heaven's name has she been
Jabb'ring on about all this time?"
"Tell you later," Bulkington said,
Watching as his leader stomped off.

Bulkington had closely followed
All the meanings he could gather
From the Nordic-sounding language
Of the lovely Queen Nokomis.
Now he'd guessed the tragic ending
Of her tale, the reason she'd stopped.
Stepping closer now he whispered,
"Tell me of your own fair daughter.
Surely there's a sweet Winona

Waiting in your village yonder?"
Oh! her eyes were so imploring
As they searched his handsome features.
"Sons I've had, three boys now banished.
Three the number of the husbands
Who have shamed me, failed the Sasquatch!
Failed to plant in me a daughter!"

Clever Bulkington did not quite
Understand the phrases uttered,
Only felt his heartbeat thudding
Felt a tide of passion rising
For this lovely, yearning creature.
Swift into his arms he swept her!
Sweet the kisses that she planted
On his face so tan and handsome.

What a sound of triumph then we

Watching warriors shouted skyward!
For another legend told us
That a tan and bearded stranger
From the portals of the sunrise,
From the land of our forefathers.
Would arrive to plant his fresh seed
In the moistly royal vessel
Of our line of queens and daughters.

Sour to the end, Sir Francis
Made a survey of the mountain,
Then his great ship pointed seaward.
Left behind, his navigator
Inland dallied in delight, and
Slept upon a royal bosom.
Lush months passed until his place was
Taken by an infant daughter.
All the air is white with moonlight,

As the three forever revel
In the mute calm of the night.

Thus a terrible cataclysm
Was averted in our kingdom.
Darker portents of the legend
Told of quaking earth and ruptures
Once the female line was ended.
Then three brothers in contention
Would devise a new beginning
To an empire torn and fractured
From the mainland. Like an island,
Floating westward, rising, sinking,
Land of Sasquatch, fate uncertain
Would into the sunset wander,
Like the new moon slowly, slowly
Sink into the purple distance.

SETTING ASIDE THE GALLEYS OF HIS LONGFELLOW MANUSCRIPT, STRETHER GOT UP AND WENT TO PEE IN THE BATHROOM.

BACK AT HIS OFFICE, THERE WAS A SURPRISE.

HEY! WHAT ARE YOU DOING HERE?

YOU' LOOK FAMILIAR.
THIS WHOLE ISSUE—A BIG MALE THING. FATHERS AND SONS, BLAH BLAH. NO STRONG WOMEN. WHERE'S YOUR FUCKING HEAD AT? AND WHAT'S THIS INDIAN CRAP?

THROW THIS SHIT IN THE TOILET. YOU WASTED WHATEVER TIME YOU SPENT ON IT.

UMPFF!

Genius foiled in truck heist

#4 Searching for Margo

[continued from p. 83]

Serial fiction by Anton Garamond

The story so far: On his way to locate someone named Margo, Luke has picked up a young woman and her baby. But now two guys are hijacking his rented truck.

Luke stepped down and faced the big Hell's Angels type. The fellow dangled the Riter truck-key and put on a moronic grin.

"Listen here—" said Luke getting out.

"It's simple," said the guy with the knit cap. "We need a truck, now we got one."

"This one's taken," declared Luke.

The big guy guffawed like an idiot. "Yeah, it's taken! Huh-huh-huh!"

"Hey, Garbage," the little guy warned his buddy. "Don't get started."

"That's his name—Garbage?"

"Yeah. He's a genius. Me? I'm Slade!" The guy actually shook Luke's hand—as if all the thugs in Oregon had good manners.

The big one still grinned, but his eyes looked wild. Now he gripped his beard with two hands and began hyperventilating.

"He's gonna have one of his spells," said Slade.

Garbage hollered at the sky, "Unscrew the locks from the doors!"

"He's quoting Whitman," said Luke.

"Sure. He's got a photographic mind.

But he's also got a short-term memory problem. You oughta see him play chess. Every move you gotta remind him whether he's playing white or black."

"Will he hurt himself?"

"Nah. He'll snap out of it."

Luke glanced at his watch.

Garbage was bent over, gagging. "Look for me under your boot-soles," he recited.

"Listen," said Luke. "I gotta deliver this ring."

"Hey, you guys—" It was Monica.

Luke's mouth actually fell open at the sight.

Garbage gripped his crotch and hollered, "Woo-Hee, girl!"

"You must work out," said Luke.

"Not really," she said. "I think it's genetic or something. Let's get going, okay?"

Luke spotted the truck-key in the dirt.

Garbage saw it, too. He lunged for it.

Luke snatched the key. "Quick, get in!" he called to Monica.

Slade leveled his silver automatic pistol. But Monica slapped his hand down. "Cut it out," she told him. "We don't want this guy's stuff. We need an empty truck. Where's our car?"

Luke stared at them. Aw, they were a team.

Monica seemed to take charge. "Okay," she told Luke. "These guys will follow us—and they'll help you unload. Then we take the truck. You report it stolen. See? Nobody gets hurt."

Luke tried to think. "Okay," he said, climbing into the truck.  He started the engine. Then he put it in gear and floored it.

The side window shattered and a bullet tore into cab's ceiling.

Luke pressed his foot to the floor, as more bullets hit the back of the truck.

"Gak-a-gurk!" squealed a voice. Oh my god, thought Luke. He'd forgotten Monica's baby. He was driving away with the baby!

[continued]

Expert learns from baby-talk

**#5 Searching
for Margo**

Serial fiction by Anton Garamond

*The story so far: To save himself from hijackers,
Luke has driven off with a young woman's baby.
He's supposed to be delivering a Hag's Ring to
someone named Margo.*

Luke hung a left, truck tires screeching. Gosh, that guy in the knit cap had fired bullets at him! The baby—thrown back and forth on the seat—looked okay.

"Gak-a-gurk," it said, sitting up.

Luke checked the rear-view mirror. If the hijackers were in a Chevy Nova, then he'd lost them.

Beyond this industrial area, downtown Portland lay somewhere to the south. Luke steered toward the sun—normally a good sign. "Fire over the Earth, the Image of Progress."

Luke was a student of signs, but these were hard times for an unemployed college English teacher. State legislators cut budgets and then boasted they'd never read Shakespeare. Surely here in Oregon, things would be different.

"Hack-a-hop," said the baby. It seemed to be staring at a blue rectangle bearing the letter H. There was a hospital ahead.

Sure, Luke decided. Drop the kid off at a hospital. Eventually Monica would locate it—if she was really the mother.

"Gak-a fis" squealed the infant. The kid actually pointed out the window at "Sweet's Market—Fresh Fish. U-Buy We Fry"

Luke glanced over. "Did you say, fish?"

The baby didn't answer. It was pulling itself up to peer out the window.

The next intersection looked ominous: Killingsworth. "Go-go-go," said the kid.

Luke dutifully stepped on the gas. At Fremont he faced a choice. Emanuel Hospital or the Fremont Bridge. Which way to Vanport University? The name hadn't seemed familiar to the waitress. Still, these warnings about Portland were adding up. They had a serious crime problem in this town.

"Bidge," said the baby.

Luke said, "Oh no. I'm going to ditch you in a nice Pediatrician's office"

"Tack-a-bidge!"

Luke felt dishearted at this turn of events. When he pictured the story of his life, he always feared he'd turn out to be a character in a dumb movie. Jeez, this better not be a talking baby.

Then he saw the bridge. Far off, beckoning above the trees: a lovely parabolic arch.

"Okay," sighed Luke and made the turn onto the winding on-ramp. Soon they were gliding up a wide highway. He glanced left for his first view of Portland's skyline. But it was hazy. As they climbed higher, the mist seemed to thicken.

"Foggy-foggy-foggy!" said the baby.

"Shut up," said Luke, slowing to a crawl. Through the haze he seemed to glimpse below a maze of wooden shanties. Then the view ahead turned blank—a terrifying whiteness.

"Oh God! I can't see the road!"

"Go-go-go!" squealed the baby.

[continued on page 116]

["Zapf-2" continued from p. 79]

You know, check her out? It took me two Ɉ7ↄɪ days to find this place."

I realized Tommy was a chump—not a killer. But I had a hunch he had other business with Culligan. "So you decided to snitch my car?" I said.

"Looks like a fast car."

"I thought car thieves went on foot."

"Yeah. But what the ɣʟc, you see a chance, you take it. Right?"

"Okay. Now, you were sent to rough up—"

Tommy looked sheepish. "I'm not supposed to tell."

"A guy in Reno," I lied, "told me it was Bill Caxton."

"Schwartz? He wouldn't hand out ʟʌcↄɪ1 like that. And who's Caxton?"

"Schwartz was at the Casino."

"Wha?" said Tommy. "He's usually at Generous Joe's."

"That's the place," I said, thinking I'd learned enough from this fumbler. He had the brain of a pancake. I let go of his ear. It looked all red and sore.

He cupped his hand over it. "You gonna let me go?" he said.

"Where can I find you?"

"I got a place in Beaverton. I'm in the phone book."

"Okay. But stay away from the lady who lives here. She doesn't want any hellos from a dead man."

"That's for J7dıℓ sure."

It was late afternoon. I should have flown my little Cessna back to Portland, because an accident on Highway 26 held me up. But it gave me time to go over things in my mind. I was on two cases: the search for a missing son and the murder of a houseman. But they both led me to Manzanita. They had to be connected—but it wasn't clear yet how or why this Wynk de Worde character was mixed up in it. Could he handle a gun? Maybe the cases were connected because both started in Manzanita forty-three years ago at a place called Smuggler's Cove.

I didn't get back to Portland's West Hills until dark. I parked in Bill Caxton's driveway and slept in my backseat.

In the morning I went in the hidden basement door, then up the stairs. I found Caxton inside, standing near his office. I figured he'd be pleased at the progress I'd made. But as I came in the door, the first words he said to me were, "<u>We don't need you anymore.</u>"

I'm a pretty tough guy, but that crack hit me like a kick in the ass.

"Oh ho!" laughed Caxton and clapped me on the shoulder. "It's good news. Wynk de Worde is my lost son! He found me. Your work is over."

"Has he got any proof?"

"You look skeptical. Of course, that's your job isn't it, to test all the facts?"

"Let me guess," I said. "He showed you a birth certificate."

"He did."

"But you know that's not proof."

Caxton folded his arms. "I'm not a fool," he said. "I have my own test. A secret code."

"Oh yeah?"

"It's something I'm sure his mother taught him—as she taught me, back in the 1950s—on the coast."

I squinted at him and said, "Maybe I could crack it."

"I doubt it," he said and unfolded a slip of paper from his wallet and handed it to me.

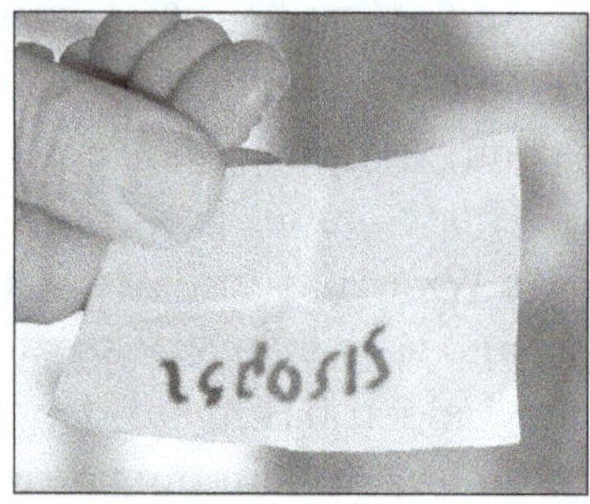

"Actually, this looks familiar."

"Oh? Then tell me what it says and what it means."

"Strether could tell you."

"Our own acting editor? That's interesting."

"Oh I get it," I said. "You showed this to Wynk. And he knew the answer. But he's seen Strether's manuscript!"

"So what?" Caxton snatched back his slip of paper.

"Strether's article about Longfellow?"

"I haven't read it."

I hadn't either, but the guy in the basement had shown me a page.

"Have you even met Strether?" Caxton demanded.

"Yeah, the other day. He's okay. Very good hearing. But he does seem a little—

"Horny?" said Caxton.

"You got it!" We both laughed.

"I hear he's cast some longing looks at my wife, Margo."

"A mighty attractive woman."

"Indeed. But with younger men, I think she prefers something a bit more— Oh, not so bookish. One might say, *dynamic?*"

"You don't mean Wynk de Worde?"

Caxton looked delighted. "It's deliciously Oedipal, isn't it?"

I winked at him, then asked, "You still got that slip of paper?"

"I carry it with me always."

"Listen," I said, glancing at a door that led to the editorial offices. "Let's corner Strether and show it to him."

"He doesn't realize I'm back in town," said Caxton. "I'm trying to keep out of the picture. "

"Aw, come-on. This'll be fun."

I found Strether sitting at a keyboard in a small room. He looked surprised to see me.

"Howdy," I said.

"Are you alone?" said Strether.

"Sort of." I knew Caxton was cooling his heels in the corridor.

"Well," he said. In his hands was the report I'd sent him two days earlier. "This document— It's quite remarkable. How did you put in the little pictures?"

"We detectives have our contacts. For instance

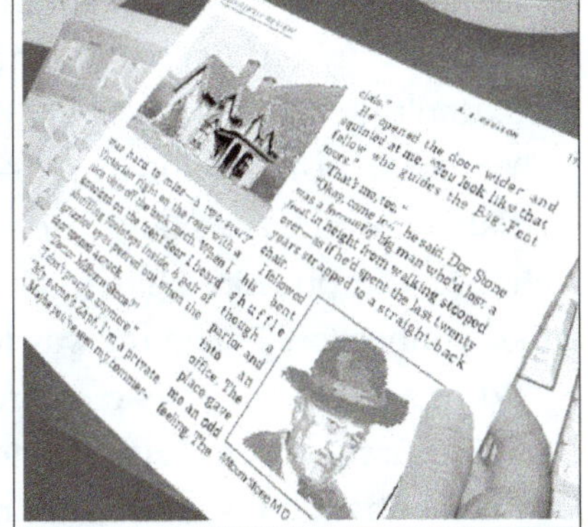

I know a guy who works at the main post office. We can get a 1st-class letter to New York in eight hours—pronto."

"Really?"

"So how are things going here?"

"Not so good. The magazine is a mess. And my personal life, well— Let's not go into that. But what you say here." He paged ahead in my report. "Birth certificates, this doctor, and a mysterious mother. I think Wynk is going to claim he's Caxton's son."

"He's already fired that shot."

"But Bill deserves better—no?"

"What do you know about this Wynk de Worde?"

"He can't be all bad—dogs seem to like him." Strether got up and shut the door. In a low voice he said, "Look here, I've got a copy of his resume. See? He spent some time in television, the weather guy in a small town. Did some summer theater, *Fiddler on the Roof, The Fantastiks*—etc. Started up several companies. It doesn't say what happened to them. Worked in a university development office, taught at a junior college, played guitar in a rock band. I think he's still looking for his niche, like an adolescent in his forties."

I pushed my hat back, singling out the key item. "It figures, don't it?"

"You mean he'll never live up to—"

"Nah, de Worde is a phony. He's acted on the stage. There's a chance someone hired him to play this part. There might be a mob connection. I'm on my way to Reno to check it out."

"What should I do?" asked Strether.

"Well, first, discourage Caxton from doing anything *loco*—like change his will. Trust me."

I went to the door and asked Caxton to step inside with his slip of paper.

"Bill!" said Strether. "You're back."

"Show him the paper," I said.

Strether examined it and smiled. "*Nokomis*," he said.

Caxton looked stunned. "And who was Nokomis?" he asked warily.

"The grandmother of Hiawatha."

"Ah ha!" laughed Caxton, relieved.

"Of course," said Strether, "there was another Nokomis."

"Another?"

"Actually, her girlhood name was, Winona. But then this handsome sailor arrived—"

"Did you learn this from your mother?"

"It's just a legend," said Strether.

Caxton's gripped his arm. "What year were you born?"

"1958. March."

"Close enough!" He pointed his finger at me. "You're back on the job, Zapf. This fellow knows more than Wynk! And you, Strether, the two of us are going to have a long talk tonight. I want to know all about you."

Caxton stormed out, eyes churning.

"What was that about?" asked Strether.

"I'll explain later. I gotta go. But here." I handed him my latest report.

"What's this paper? Hey, here's a picture of Bill."

"Finger-click it," said Zapf.

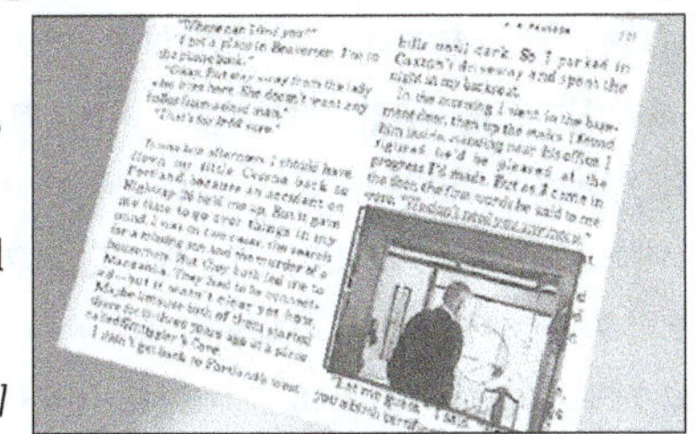

[To "Zapf's Report #3" p. 142]

The Editor's Column Part IV

A week passed. Zapf wrote from a hospital in Reno to say that gangsters had beaten him up. He enclosed a picture an orderly took of him.

On my end, Wynk and I nearly came to blows. We hadn't actually spoken much lately.

And some woman keeps calling me on the phone. Maybe Marilee from Minneapolis? She started this foolish chastity business and told me not to answer the phone. Witness my loins clammering with desire. And then there's Monica—that character with the baby—who'd shown up to critique my Longfellow article (see p. 100).

But this ringing, this calling, has jarred loose old obsessions. I was on a quest—for what? The ungraspable something. Surely that was a dream.

Consider this: if you're asleep and a text presents itself which resists the act of reading, then you know you're dreaming. Syllables blur and congeal into nonsense. It's the same with trying to write. So remember this: feel yourself on the verge of falling asleep. Now imagine taking up a pencil and jotting down a thought. If you're over the edge, you'll only manage a letter or two—then <u>things will whirl</u> and spin off into oblivion!

So, evidently, I'm awake here. These manuscripts piled up on my desk, I heft them like bricks. Their prose is brassy, mawkish. The thin stuff of genre-fiction is invading *The American Quarterly Review*. Gosh, I have unpublished stories that are better than this cheap fusion of magic, sci-fi, and romance.

Now about that fight I had with Wynk. He's selling whole pages for advertising space. But it's my job to keep the magazine from being dumbed-down. I raised this issue when I found him on the deck scratching Bill's Lab.

He looked up from the dog, said, "You're a ʃ7ↄɪℓ literary hack.

"You're a ʃↄ٦ɓɪↄʌↄ boob," I replied. "You don't resemble Bill."

"ↄɩɪ, this job is your fate, Strether."

That silenced me. The notion that things might be determined, charted out in advance, has always chilled me. I imagine a ruthless mechanism shuttling through strict permutations,

[continued from p. 42]

In the classic sestina, the terminal words of each stanza are the same, but their order is rearranged.

An example: Sydney's, "Ye Goatherd Gods":

1

Ye Goatherd gods, that love the grassy mountains,
Ye nymphs which haunt the springs in pleasant valleys,
Ye satyrs joyed with free and quiet forests,
Vouchsafe your silent ears to plaining music,
Which to my woes gives still and early morning,
And draws the dolor on till weary evening.

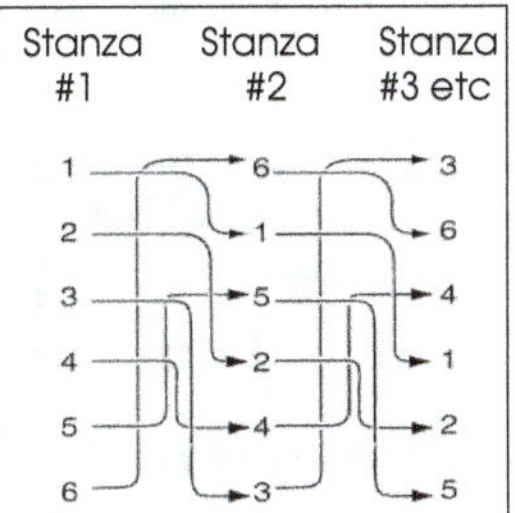

2

O Mercury, foregoer to the evening,
O heavenly huntress of the savage mountains,
O lovely star, entitled of the morning,
While that my voice doth fill these woeful valleys,
Vouchsafe, your silent ears to plaining music
Which oft hath echo tired in secret forests.

[Strether]

merely to tantalize us with novelties. The mind of God, a supercomputer—either one can probably slap together keen moments of an entire lifetime, one's triumphs and shameful secrets, epiphany announced without a by-stander to share it. And it boils down to? A shuffling of items in an algorithm. Back in the days when you could trust Alan Watts—before he dropped all that acid—it was reassuring to know that Fate wasn't a problem if the Self being pushed around was a fiction. In Oregon, of all places, you'd think the grassy love gods still leapt to the music of Norman O. Brown.

Anyway, Wynk and I didn't come to blows. I shook my frail fist in his face and said, "The problem with you is, you think you're a commodity." [continued on p. 120]

[Sestina]

Now, Isaac Moore's great breakthrough was to ask whether this vertical pattern might be applied *horizontally*. Of course, the permutation shuffles only six items—in a poem, a six word line. And what comes next? You ask a good question: *the same six words.* Let's try condensing a line from Sir Philip Sidney and indicating where the words would fall in the next line:

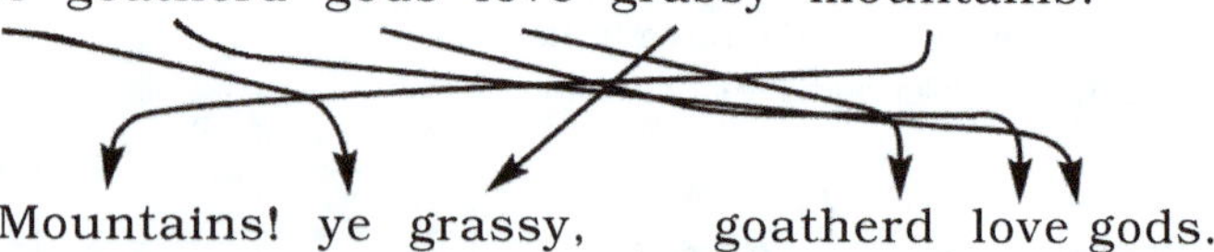

Now we're ready to face the full intensity of Isaac Moore's "Minimal Double Sestina," six stanzas ordered by *both* a vertical and horozontal permutation. Because Moore chose a quotation from Stein for the first line, we hear Hemingstraining to mock her syntax while he weaves in his own bleak obsession with *Nada*:

Minimal Double Sestina
by Isaac Moore

1

"Ernest, remarks are not literature." —Stein
Stein: "Ernest, literature remarks, '*Not* are.'"
"Are, Stein, not earnest remarks, literature?"
"Literature are!" remarks Stein Ernestnot.
"Not literature, Ernest, are *Stein-remarks*.
Remarks (not *Stein-literature*) are earnest."

2

"*Stein-literature* not are?" remarks Ernest.
"Literature are earnest remarks. Not Stein,
not Ernest, are *Stein-literature-remarks*."
"Remarks (not literature), Ernest Stein, are
earnest *Stein-remarks*." "Literature are *Not*.
Are remarks, Stein, not earnest literature?"

3

"Earnest remarks (not Stein) are literature,"
remarks Stein, "Literature are *not* earnest."
"Literature," Ernest remarks, "are *Stein-not*."
"Are not remarks literature, Ernest Stein?"
"Not literature? Stein! Ernest! Remarks are!"
"Stein are earnest," *Not-literature* remarks.

4

"Not Stein, *literature*, Ernest. Are remarks,
remarks not? Are Stein, Ernest, literature?"
"Literature," remarks Ernest (not Stein), *are*."
"Are literature," Stein remarks, "not earnest?"
"Ernest are not literature," remarks Stein.
"Stein," Ernest remarks, "are literature *Not*?"

5

Ernest remarks, "Literature are *Stein-not*"
"Are Stein, earnest literature, not re-marks?"
"Literature. Not. Are. Ernest," remarks Stein
(not Ernest). Stein remarks, "Are literature
re-marks? Are not *Stein-literature* earnest?"
Stein-literature re-marks *Not*." ("Ernest are.")

6

"*Not?*" remarks Literature. "*Stein, Ernest, are*."
Remarks Stein, "Are earnest literature not?
Literature are Stein (not re-marks), Ernest-
Stein! (Ernest-Not-literature!)" "Are remarks—
are not earnest remarks—*Stein-literature?*"
"Earnest literature-re-marks are *not* Stein."

White-out on Fremont Bridge

#6 Searching for Margo  *[continued from p. 105]*

Serial fiction by Anton Garamond

The story so far: Hurrying to locate Vanport University—
and deliver a ring to someone named Margo—Luke and
a strange baby face disaster crossing the river.

I can't see the road!" remarked Luke. "Go-go," said the baby. This annoying gibberish hammered at Luke's ears. Had accepting Olga's ring sent him over the edge? Crazy stuff. Auditory hallucinations.

"We'll go over the side!" he yelled.

"Uppy-uppy!" cried the kid.

Puppy? guppy? wondered Luke. Then he leaned to look up—as if up to Heaven—through the windshield. Overhead, blue sky, an American flag, and the arches of the bridge were perfectly visible. And his Riter truck was aligned just right.

"Go-go!" repeated the baby.

Luke accelerated into the white fog. Then he slammed on the brakes. He'd almost rear-ended a horse-drawn wagon!

The baby was thrown forward, but instantly scrambled back onto the seat.

Luke glared at the kid. "Go? You can't even see over the dashboard."

They reached the top and headed down through thinning haze. A blue H directed him left on 23rd, a muddy road. At Lovejoy he stopped in front of the hospital, a big white Victorian with a cupola, end chimneys, and a massive front porch. It didn't look like a modern institution. But the name was perfect: *Good Samaritan Hospital and Orphanage.* He'd leave the kid here and be on his way.

As Luke climbed out with the baby, an old geezer stopped to stare. "Got a girl in trouble?" he cried, slapping his knee.

"No, actually—" said Luke.

A big nurse in a starched apron came down from the porch. "We don't want trouble," she said.

Luke wasn't sure he could explain. He thrust out the baby like a gift.

"Poo-poo on yew!" said the infant.

The nurse's broad Irish face turned beet red. "Who said that?" she asked.

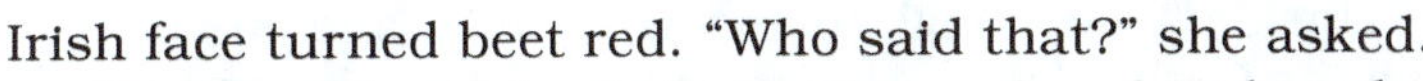

Now an old coot in clerical collar and a white beard came charging out of the orphanage.

Women in a full skirts and bonnets paused to gawk. Gosh, thought Luke, these were really authentic costumes. And the sidewalk was made of wood. Luke decided he'd stumbled upon Oregon Trail Dress-up Day in Portland.

"Abomination!" yelled the Reverend.

The commotion created a traffic-jam of horses and buggies on 23rd Street. Men in suspenders shook their fists. They stared at his yellow Riter Truck as if it were some huge device about to explode. Luke heard a whistle that might signify the arrival of the police.

"Lez git," advised the baby.

Luke climbed back into the truck. He considered asking them what century they were in. But instead he yelled, "Where can I buy diapers?"

"Fred Meyer!" the crowd hollered, as if their voices were a gramophone recording.

[continued]

Sleazy offer at Fred Meyer

**#7 Searching
for Margo**

Serial fiction by Anton Garamond

*The story so far: Luke found horses and buggies on
NW 23rd street, but has failed to abandon the baby.
He's still hurrying deliver a ring to someone at Van-
port University.*

The smell of horse manure disappeared when Luke's
yellow, Riter truck reached Fred Meyer's on Burnside.

"Sorry, little guy," he told the baby. "I'm trying to take
care of you, but I'm imagining a lot of weird things."

Inside, Luke bought diapers, formula, and jars bearing the Gerber label. As if from a list, the baby had
seemed to call out the items it wanted.

In line at the cash registers, Luke slipped Olga's ring
off his little finger. When she told him to deliver it to Portland, there'd been a terrible urgency in her voice. He'd actually been hurrying for two days now, aiming to avert
some ambiguous disaster. For example, what would this
Margo-person do—drink Draino?—if he was late delivering
the ring? And what about that zany threat: cutting off his
wiener?

He'd brushed close to disaster himself today. It was
crazy to think the ring was magic. But without it would
he be dead in the Columbia river, full of bullet holes, or
still falling off the Fremont Bridge?

Just now the baby snatched the ring and popped it
into his mouth!

"Gimme that!" Luke demanded.

"Funf-phooey," said the baby.

Luke pried open its jaws.

"Oh, sir!" said an indignant woman behind him.

Luke grinned. "Say something cute for the lady. Like
your comments on the semiotics of shopping."

As the baby let out a gob of drool, the woman frowned and took a step back.

"Vanport!" announced Luke brightly, holding out the ring. "I gotta find somebody who works there."

From the next check-out lane, an old guy called out, "Vanport? It washed away in the big flood."

Luke slapped his forehead. "A flood?"

City of Portland (OR) Archives. A2004-002.867

"Yup. Twenty thousand homeless. Fifteen dead. Mostly black folks."

"So," said Luke. "I didn't make it here in time."

"I guess not. It happened in 1948."

This news didn't help. Luke went out to the truck perplexed. Why had that waitress given him the name of a universiy that no longer existed?

The baby had fallen asleep. Luke laid it on the truck seat and eased the passenger door shut.

An unshaven fellow leaned against a dumpster. "Got a fertilizer bomb in that Riter truck?" the guy joked.

"Is that what people think? They're giving me wrong directions. To Vanport, for instance."

"Right up the hill. Look for the sign that says, Pittock—" Suddenly the guy clammed up.

Luke stared at him. "Pittock?"

"Nice little baby you got there," drawled the fellow. "Is it for sale?"

"Why would I want to sell my baby?"

"Well—" The fellow rubbed his chin. "First, it's not your baby. Or you'd have one of those car-seats for it. Second, you got bullet holes in your truck. And third, I know a guy who'll give you ten thousand dollars for it. What do you say?"

[continued on page 126]

[Strether: continued from p. 114]

He gave me one of his cheesy, Development Office smiles. "Hey," he said. "Let's work this out."

"Okay. Stop selling my space?"

"Judicious placement."

"What's that?"

"That's the solution. The ads will go where they won't interfere with your articles, stories—whatever."

"You agree they won't distract from texts that have real literary merit?

"Exactly. "

"That sounds fair," I said, leaning on the deck rail-

Killarney, the Ring of Kerry, Tralee, Dublin.
Your host: Prof. Molly Darcy, Yeats Expert,
Donegal University.

Ethel's Travel Shoppe
Multnomah Village, OR

ing and gazing out at the forested view. "You know, Wynk, sometimes you're okay. I know we didn't hit it off when I first got here—" I glanced back. He was gone. This has happened before. He seems to vaporize, to come and go like some visitor from another dimension.

Then, through the big windows, I spotted him inside the house. Margo Caxton appeared. The two greeted one another. Then he seized her in a tight embrace. A spike of jealousy rose up in my chest and skewered my heart. Who was she to him?

I hadn't really taken Zapf and his theories seriously. Now the poor old guy, on the trail of some hallucination, was hospitalized down in Reno. He reminded me of Gregory Corso, who used pick fights in bars—and get beaten up.

But standing there on the deck, bitterness streaming and clotting within me, I sided with Zapf. Wynk was some kind of con-man, an imposter, come down from Bellingham, via Manzanita, to horn in not only on the magazine but Caxton's name, fortune, who knows what else?

As I watched Margo laugh and push him away, I

realized that she might become—if Wynk had his way—his stepmother. So any hanky-panky between the two was out of the question. Unless— Oh god. Unless— *She was part of it.* The two of them. Plotting to wrest control of the magazine from poor, aging Bill Caxton.

Attention
to Detail

Alexander
Phemister

Certified
Public
Accountants
PDX, Oregon

As I watched, Margo cast her famous gray eyes in my direction. Seeing me peering in at the window, she came hurrying out to the deck.

"Oh, Strether," she said. "I'm so sorry I got you mixed up in this." And she touched my cheek with her slender fingers.

I lost myself in the warmth of her touch, and imagined myself gliding up her tawny thighs, approaching the gateway to—

"Mixed up in what?" I said.

"Well, now that you're a *candidate*—"

"Oh?"

"Listen. I only knew that Bill had a thing about those old names: *Nokomis* and *Winona.* I assumed it was Longfellow he was obsessing about. So to

humor him, after I heard your paper at the MLA, it seemed like such a— Such a cute idea. To invite you out here. But now it's gotten out of hand, don't you think? I mean, your being a candidate?"

I looked into her eyes and felt encircled by radiance. "Of course. But a candidate for . . ."

"For being *his long-lost son!* Bill told me all about the chat you had last week. You know, about what's-her-name—Winona, or somebody?"

"It's just a legend," I said.

"Not according to Bill."

"Well. He was intensely curious. But not about me, exactly."

"Oh, he's very fond of you."

"That's nice to hear. But see— Okay. He asked a lot of questions about where I grew up, and did my mother tell me about Nokomis, and so forth. But I had to tell him: I've got a father already. And I love him dearly, even if he can't talk anymore. Can't walk either. And I hope they don't mistreat him at the nursing home."

Margo was examining me, her eyes brooding.

"So," I said. "I'm not mixed up in this. I've simply got a job to do here."

"You work too hard," she said. "Have you been out much? Seen the city? There's lots to see. So much dense history here—almost back to Lewis and Clark."

I didn't tell her there were several characters I didn't want to run into off these grounds. On the other hand, there was my old quest...

"It's a long walk," I finally said.

"Of course. You don't have a car! How could we have been so thoughtless?" She was wearing a cashmere cardigan that had pockets. Out of one she drew a single key and held it out.

"Car?" I said.

"The VW. Can you drive a stick- shift?"

"Sure. But—"

"I insist," she said.

Ten minutes later I was behind the wheel of a vintage Beetle with a Porsche engine, wondering if someone had just shoved me out of the house.

But it was a glorious day, and it felt fine to coast down the long gravel drive. Fine to leave behind my little cubicle, the keyboards and monitors. Well— Okay. Workaholic that I was, I'd thrown a file folder of my own old manuscripts into the trunk, thinking there's be a wooded glen to stretch out and revise a few pages—

What's this? I asked myself on the main road. A sign pointed to somebody's mansion. Who could resist? I pulled a sharp left and followed the <u>roadway up-hill</u>. It wound past large estates and fi-nally landed me in front of the thing. Jeez, who could afford to wash all those windows?

I backed the VW into a parking area. The only other ve-hicle there was a big yellow truck.

A shaggy looking character came out of the woods and stared at Margo's car. "That ain't no slug-bug," he said.

"It belongs to a friend of mine," I told him. He seemed to be wearing too many layers of clothing.

"Whatcha got in there?" He was peering in the windows.

"Not much. What do you know about this place?"

"Some rich bastard built it. I take a class here. Want to hear about it?"

"Not really." I walked over and read the plaque about Pit-tock. Then I cir-cled around to the other side of the place and encountered a surprise…

["Editor-4" continued on p. 130]

Locals spurn newcomer

#8 Searching
for Margo

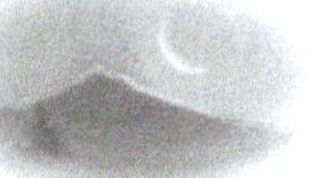

[continued from p. 119]

Serial fiction by Anton Garamond

The story so far: In NW Portland, a fellow has offered to buy the baby. But he's also mentioned the name, 'Vanport,' where Luke hopes to locate the mysterious Margo

Luke said, "Ten thousand dollars?" A dirty face popped up in the dumpster. The guy had a banana peel on his head. "Fifteen thousand!" he shouted.

His friend swatted him back down. "That includes our share, you idiot. Now shut up!"

Luke made a note that one fellow wore boots and the other a plaid shirt. Back East, people pictured everyone in Oregon dressing this way.

"Tell you what," the unshaven fellow was saying. "I got two hundred pounds of copper wire in the woods. Help me haul it to salvage, I'll give you five dollars."

"Okay," said Luke. "And you tell me what you were saying about Vanport being just up the hill."

"You musta misunderstood me." The fellow's eyes had gone blank again.

"Then," said Luke, "I got no time to haul wire."

The guy in the dumpster popped up looking aghast. "No time for recycling?"

"It don't sound like he's from Oregon."

"Oh my gosh. A new-comer?"

"I bet he's from— California!"

Both fellows covered their eyes in mock horror and peeped out between their dirty fingers.

Luke climbed in his rented Riter truck and started the engine. It was still hard for him to say *no* to people who asked for help. As he drove off he heard them hollering, "J7d‚ Out-of-Stater!"

Luke followed the street called 'Burnside' until it went uphill. Now the noise of city traffic lay behind him. Forested slopes, tangled in vines, tilted up from the roadway. Then he spotted it: an arrow for "Pittock Mansion." He hung a sharp right and climbed still higher.

Eventually he reached a parking lot where people were getting into cars and tour busses. It was just after four o'clock. The place was closing down.

On the seat beside him, the baby lay curled in sleep. Could he risk leaving it alone for ten minutes? He put a jacket over the kid, and got out.

Past a stone carriage house he could see a large building: tiled roofs, four or more chimney's, enormous

leaded glass windows. If this was a university, then he'd found the Administration Building.

Someone who looked like a cleaning woman got into the last car and drove off. Luke had the sinking feeling that he was late again.

But here came a lovely young woman. She carried a

wooden sign. Hefting it up, she fastened it on top of a tilted plaque. Hers read: Vanport University.

"Excuse me?" said Luke.

Seeing him, the woman dashed away!

"Wait!" cried Luke. And then, on impulse, he called out, "Margo!"

She stopped and looked back. But on her stunning face was a look of panic. And again she fled.

[continued]

College for the homeless

#9 Searching
for Margo

Serial fiction by Anton Garamond

The story so far: At the Pittock Mansion, Luke has found a woman posting a sign for Vanport University. Could she be the mysterious Margo he's come so far to find?

Luke watched the young woman round the corner of the big stone building. "Margo, come back!" he called. But she was gone.

He walked to his truck, thinking he'd come back tomorrow. He should find a place to stay, unload his stuff, and— Gosh, he felt so— What? So *unsure.*

Luke got in behind the wheel. The baby was awake and asked, "Did you find her?"

Luke ignored this talk, But it was becoming interesting, this hallucination.

"You suspect she'll turn out to be pretty. Jeez, not smart, clever, or resourceful. Just pretty."

Luke decided he was projecting unconscious conflicts onto to the kid so he could read them back. Baby Rorschach. But how explain driving all the way from Minnesota with only a name to go on? *Margo.* And why had he hollered it at an attractive stranger and scared her away?

The baby glanced at the stone carriage house. "We'd better check this place out," the baby said.

"I gotta sleep," said Luke. Ah, to sleep—perchance to dream. Was this the undiscovered country? He grabbed a diaper, a bottle, and carried the kid back to where he'd lost sight of the young woman.

"Around the corner," said the baby.

Luke followed a stone terrace. The views on this side of the building were terrific. And here was a line of people— unshaven men, a woman with her shopping cart full of plastic bags. Each was dangling a penny at the end of a thread.

Supervising them was an old guy in a white lab coat. His spectacles and white goatee made him look like an anorexic Colonel Sanders. When he spotted Luke, he glared at him and said, "Vhat's this? A schtudent late to class?"

"Actually—" said Luke.

"You gott your penny?"

"I'm simply looking for—"

"Silence! The experiment is undervay!"

Luke and the baby took a position next to a dirty fellow who actually smelled okay. "Is this the university?" whispered Luke.

"This is String Theory / Seismology 103," said the guy.

"Earthquakes?"

"Volcanoes, too. See, it's all connected. Underground."

"Where are the rest of the university buildings?"

"This is it."

"Who's the guy in the lab-coat?"

"Professor Overton. Or maybe it's Overtone?"

"Shush back there!" said the professor. "Now, observe your penny. It twirls. Vait. It stops, no? Now tell me, vhat's facing you—heads or tails?"

The line of students all called out "Tails."

Ridiculous, thought Luke.

"Ja," said the professor. "The head of the coin has the greater mass, no? It seeks the volcanic magma working its vay up through the earth! Look!". He was pointing out over the trees, over the Portland skyline at Mt. Hood.

[continued on page 132]

["Editor-4" continued from page 125]

. . . a veranda. ringed by a concrete balustrade. There was

some litter I picked up. And an old bent copper penny: 1958 D. The veranda faced an enormous lawn. I walked out to the center. Through trees you could make out the whole city—Mt. Hood in the hazy distance.

If only I'd brought a camera. The view back to the house was pretty in-spiring—if the rewards of capitalist enterprise inspire you. Still, I knew the fellow's name now: Pittock.   And   inside they'd have preserved the residue of his life:

furnishings, family pictures—guides leading visitors from room to room, relating tragic anecdotes. It amounted to a kind of immortality.

Monuments like this one—revisiting the past in general—provoke these maudlin moods in me. This whole Caxton business—me trying to edit a literary journal—is it what I was placed on this earth to accomplish? Better to build in stone, or write a powerful rhyme.

Back at the parking lot, I was surprised to see the front hood of Margo's VW standing open. Someone had levered it open with a crow-bar! And inside, my manu-scripts were gone!

The big yellow truck still sat next to the VW. Feet were

Feet were sticking out near the back wheels. On the asphalt lay two empty 40-ounce beer bottles.

I crouched down and saw a shaggy guy, passed out. There were no manuscripts in sight. He opened his eyes when I shook his leg.

"Who did this to my car?" I said.

"Wha's-a-matter?" he said.

"Somebody stole my stuff. You must have seen them."

"We don't steal from each other."

"Give me a break."

He crawled out from under the truck. "You look like a rich bastard to me," he said. "Got a nice house?"

"I don't have a house."

"You don't look homeless."

That made me think. "In a way, I guess I am."

"Ever been on the road?"

"Yup."

"Hungry? In despair about how you fucked-up your life?"

"That's me," I said.

"O.K. Then you're one of us. I'll see what I can do."

The guy actually had a cell-phone in his backpack. As he went around to the back of the truck, he was punching in a number. When he came back he was all smiles.

"We know who's got the stolen property," he said.

"Really."

"A guy named Teddy—missing two front teeth. Your papers are in his book-bag. He's headed for the Park Blocks for his afternoon nap."

"What do I do? Get a cop?"

"Hell. Just tell him he made a mistake."

[continued on p. 134]

Mt. Hood eruption due?

#10 Searching for Margo

[continued from p. 129]

Serial fiction by Anton Garamond

The story so far: On the terrace of the Pittock Mansion, Luke and the baby have found not Margo but Prof. Overton teaching homeless people about String Theory.

Everyone looked again at the coins they dangled from threads. Sure enough, tails faced them, heads pointed to Mt. Hood. "Professor," asked the bag-lady with the shopping cart. "Could ya explain that again?"

"Consult your notes vor the mass of Mt. Hood!"

The lady shuffled through a wad of notes written on paper towels from a public restroom, then recited: "One hundred twenty-two billion tons."

"Und what did the great Isaac Newton say?"

She squinted at another page: "Bodies attract one another with a force directly proportional to the product of their masses and inversely proportional to the square of the distance between them."

"So even a tiny variation in the mass of one side of a coin might—?

"Oh!" Her face glowed with the thrill of intellectual discovery. "You gotta multiply by billions!"

"Listen," said Luke impatiently. "I've driven all the way from Minnesota to find Margo."

Overton's spectacles flashed at him like blank disks. "How do you know Margo?"

"I don't. That's the problem."

"Ah, the problem is that a hundert years ago a similar coin pointed at Mt. St. Helens! There the volcanic magma vas gathering until—"

"Until 1981," said the unshaven fellow next to Luke. "I saw that one blow."

"Und give magma an underground nudge from the Tillamook continental plate—poof!"

The class, visibly shaken, all stared at Mt. Hood.

"Now, in 1845," said the professor, "there was a famous coin twirling."

A hand went up. "Lovejoy and Pettygrove flipped a coin," said a bright, filthy student,

"Ja. But they didn't flip a coin to name the city Portland or Boston. They *twirled* it. And the winner knew which way heads would face."

"Who knew the gravitational secret?" asked the bag-lady.

"Francis Pettygrove," said the professor bitterly. "Can you guess who taught him the trick?"

These names meant nothing to Luke. But it had sounded as if this insane Professor might know Margo.

Just now a bent old lady was handing out cardboard 3-D glasses. She gave a pair to Luke and flashed him a toothless smile.

"It's time to clear you minds for a zientific zimulation," announced the Professor. "Don't think about magma! Don't think about coins twirling!"

Everyone put on their glasses and stood hushed as the professor clicked a TV remote at the horizon.

They had a clear view of Mt. Hood. In slow motion, the

sharp top of the mountain seemed to shatter. Pieces rose in the air followed by billowing smoke! The plume went up and up. It was coming this way! <u>Mt. Hood was exploding</u>. And big chunks were going to fall on the city Portland!"

[continued on page 136]

[continued from p. 131]

"What if he doesn't believe me?"

"Then do the Hobo-handshake."

"What if I forgot how?"

The shaggy guy narrowed his eyes. "Kinda sour, aren't-cha? You sure you been on the road?"

"It starts like this, right?" Brightly, I offered my hand and he took it.

"That's it. Now slide back, curl your fingers. Good. Make a fist. Knock. Now open your hand. Get a gob of phlegm up from your throat—" The guy hacked and spit something on his palm.

"I forgot this part," I said, spitting.

"You're joshin' me. Now we shake again. That's it—goo it around. And now the finale." The guy slapped his knee with his gooey hand and let out a shrill Yee-Haw! "That's it. Well, you could do a little jig if the spirit moves you. That's when you're seeing the bright side of things. And you know what they say? They say the Hobo-handshake brings luck."

"Luck," I said. "I could use some of that."

The guy gave me directions to the Park Blocks and Teddy's nap bench. Twenty minutes later I explored a block-wide swath of trees and grass that ran past the Art Museum. Office workers found it a nice place to sit and eat lunch. On a few benches, ragged fellows sprawled asleep. I went from one to the next, whispering, "Teddy?" They stirred and said a word or two, giving me a glimpse of their front teeth.

At last I think I found my man. Hearing the name, *Teddy*, he jolted up. I said, "Want some cheese?"

"Cheese?" he said, showing a black gap.

"Where are my papers?" I demanded. "You made a mistake. And I want them back. Wanna do the Hobo-Handshake?"

"The one where you spit? Man, nobody ever did that."

"But my stuff!" I hollered.

"Yeah, from the VW? I sold those papers to the Wild Man."

"Where do I find him?"

"He comes and goes."

"What does he look like?

"You can't miss him. Big beard, scraggly hair. Runs around naked."

"I'll probably spot him."

"Nah. He disappears. Hard to find."

That intrigued me. But I had to park Margo's VW and check out things that I'd seen on a map. <u>Pioneer Square</u>, was worth a visit and then a waterfall fountain.

[continued on p. 142]

Residents fear the Big One

#11 Searching for Margo

[continued from p. 133]

Serial fiction by Anton Garamond

The story so far: From the Pittock Mansion terrace, Professor Overton is letting his homeless students see Mt. Hood erupt. And he seems to know who Margo is.

Luke watched the huge plume rising over the Portland skyline. The debris from Mt. Hood would bury the city under tons of hot dust! Crowds would run down narrow city streets as the billowing gray cloud roiled behind them. Luke <u>ripped off his cardboard 3-D glasses</u>. Everything seemed dim until he realized his eyes were closed. He blinked and saw the mountain back in place, radiant in clear afternoon sunlight.

In a line, the others stood, mouths agape. Some raised their hands to fend off what they were seeing. An unshaven guy fell to his knees in prayer.

"Off with the glasses!" ordered the professor.

"Look at those chumps," said the baby. "They look like zombies."

"Did you see it?" stammered Luke. "Without wearing glasses?"

"I imagined it. Just like you did."

"You will feel refreshed and eager to do your home-work," the professor was telling his class. "Bring three Popsicle schticks to class for tomorrow's experiment."

The toothless old lady collected the 3-D glasses, and

the destitute members of String Theory/Semiology 103
stumbled off to trails in the woods.

"Are you crazy?" said Luke, approaching Prof. Overton.

"Feel less nervous now? Having seen it?"

"I don't know what you did—virtual reality, I guess—
but you scared the shit out of those people."

"So," smiled Overton. "It's therapy."

"The sign says there's a university here."

Overton spread his arms wide. "Ja, right here. Vanport.
A brand new university for Portland!"

"And for students, you've got these—" Luke glanced at
the professor's toothless old lady assistant and lowered his
voice. "—these community people?"

"The disinherited. You gott to start somewhere."

"Ask him about Margo," whispered the baby.

The professor ignored the infant on Luke's hip. "Let me
guess," he said. "You're an academic?"

"I've taught some college," conceded Luke. "But I'm new
in town."

"Ah. Then you're not worried about the Big One. To you
the phrase is familiar?"

Luke shook his head.

"Picture San Francisco at the turn of the zentury. A
glittering jewel on the west coast. And the better it gets, the
more people worry."

"So that's what everyone in Portland is worried about? "

"Ja. About the Big One. An earthquake! On the coast
comes a tsunami—a thousand feet high. But can you picture it? Of course not. *Der Erstuß*—the shaking, makes
only a big blur. *Und untergrund* the plates squeeze the
magma upwards. Dormant volcanoes all around here."

"So you simulate a volcanic eruption? And you claim
you can predict both with a penny on a string?"

Overton shrugged. "String Theory says that gravity is
the vortex to other dimensions."

"Like alternate universes?"

"You might be in several right now."

[continued]

Portland weather changes

#12 Searching for Margo

Serial fiction by Anton Garamond

*The story so far: Luke and the talking baby have
heard Professor Overton explain Portland's fears
about the Big One. He also claims that gravity is the
vortex to other dimensions.*

They stood there on the terrace of the Pittock Mansion.
Luke glanced up at the massive stone building rising
behind them. "Okay," he said. "So this university you're
starting—Vanport—it's brand new. And this is your building?"

Overton was squinting up at a cloud in the sky.

"Inside you've got classrooms?" asked Luke. "Probably
labs and offices?"

"Oh, this was Pittock's place. The bastard. I'm just bor-
rowing the terrace—after they close up. Usually we meet
unter a bridge. That's where I've been recruiting my schtu-
dents." The professor sighed. "You gott to start somewhere."

The Baby tugged at the ring on Luke's finger and whispered, "Ask him about Margo. And that pretty woman we
saw putting up the sign."

"So, you've taught college?" Overton asked.

"A couple places back east," said Luke. "It's hard to get
tenure anywhere these days."

"Then you have a Ph.D. In History, perhaps?" The man
was staring at him with fiendish intensity. Overhead, the
sky was getting oddly dark.

"English literature," said Luke.

"Close enough. You must have contacts. You must know

people. Ja, a genuine academic. And you're here for the interview!"

"Interview?" said Luke.

"To join my faculty!"

"Actually," said Luke. "I'm looking for this person. Someone told me she works here at Vanport."

Just then, large drops of rain began spattering the terrace.

'You wouldn't mind starting at the rank of Instructor?"

"Listen, I saw a young woman earlier. She seemed to stop when I called the name, *Margo*. I've got something to give her."

The professor took Luke aside and lowered his voice. "This is a delicate subject. We're not even sure that Margo is still alive."

"Oh no," sighed Luke. "She's dead?" Was he late after all? Now the rain came down hard. They were getting

drenched.

"Of course," the professor went on, "I can give you certain information."

"Do you realize it's raining?" remarked Luke.

"Vhat's the matter," said Overton. "You don't like Portland weather?"

The professor yanked Luke and the baby to the other end of the terrace. Here was a bright patch of sunlight. The flagstones underfoot were perfectly dry.

"Now about Margo," said Overton. "I have certain information."

Luke was sopping wet, as if he'd stepped into a pool where the answers to all his questions simply floated about within reach. "Information?" he said. "Like what?"

"I can tell you where to find her."

[continued]

Rare coin to be presented

#13 Searching
for Margo

Serial fiction by Anton Garamond

*The story so far: Professor Overton has asked Luke
to join the faculty at Vanport University—whose students are homeless. But Margo might not be alive.*

Luke tried to read the expression behind the professor's
spectacles. "Come on," said Luke. "This Margo is dead,
but you'll tell me where to find the corpse?"

"In a sense," nodded Overton.

Luke was exasperated. Had he come this far only to be
confronted by riddles?

"I'm asking you to do me a favor," said Overton. "Join my
faculty, I'll tell you about Margo. Ja?"

Luke had never been offered a college teaching position
so fast. But he was tired, sleep-deprived, disoriented.

"Take the job," whispered the baby.

"Okay," Luke told the Professor. Probably they needed
someone to teach a section of Freshman Composition. "When
do I start?" he asked.

"Right now. I need you to make a delivery. You recall the
twirling coins that stopped facing Mt. Hood?"

"Right, you said someone named *Pettygrove* knew the
trick. But I doubt he Scotch-taped a thread to a penny in
1845."

"Precizely! He used this one." Overton
drew out a bronze Chinese coin with a
square hole in the middle. A bit a old
string was tied through the hole.

"Wow," said the baby.

"This is the very coin that Asa Lovejoy

(may he burn in hell) und Francis Pettygrove (the scoundrel) twirled to name the city either Boston or Portland. I want you to present this rare coin to the Oregon Historical Soziety. It's right downtown."

"Sounds easy," said Luke. "But why me?"

"Because you've gott credentials! You've gott the Ph.D. Academic connections. You they'll believe!" The professor handed Luke an old letter and a small glass rectangle. It

was a daguerreotype. If he tilted it the right way in the sun Luke could make out a figure dangling something in the air.

"And this is Lovejoy or Pettygrove?"

"It's my grandfather, *William Overton.*"

"He was German."

"No no! But he's the key to everything. Now be careful! This plate and the letter are priceless historical artifacts. They're connected with the coin."

The bent old woman came over. "How do you know you can trust this guy?" she snarled. Luke wondered if the old bat was Overton's wife.

The professor blinked. "That's a gut question." He seemed to be reconsidering the entire—somewhat hasty—proposition.

"Hey," whispered the baby. "I got a plan. Leave me here."

"I couldn't do that, " said Luke

"Men!" muttered the old woman. "Who could trust a *man?*"

"Wah!" cried the baby. It held its arms out to the toothless lady.

"What's this?" she said, her creased face softening as she accepted the kid. Her hair hung down in a curtain of greasy tangles.

Luke decided he deserved a time-out from the kid. But it would feel odd to leave him behind. "Take care," he said.

[continued on page 150]

["Editor-4" continued from p. 135]

At Keller Fountain, Zapf looked a little wet after emerging from behind the waterfall.

"How are you?" I asked. The knuckles of his hands were wrapped in surgical tape.

"I jump around to keep in shape," he said. "But they smacked the daylights outta me in Reno."

"They?"

"You better read my latest Report." Zapf handed me a sheaf of papers. I flipped through it, looking for little pictures. But I didn't see any.

"Hey," I said. "This is quite a coincidence, running into you here."

He looked disappointed. "You didn't know I was tailing you?" he said.

"Really?"

"Starting at the Pittock place. Sorry, I didn't catch that

["Editor-4" continued on the next page]

["Zapf" continued from p. 111]

Zapf's Third Report

After getting Strether and Caxton together about that Nokomis business, I found Gordon Sable and Wynk de Worde out on the deck. They were arguing.

"Howdy," I said.

Sable gave me a neutral look. "I thought your work was over."

"Your buddy Caxton decided to keep me on the case."

De Worde put on a phony grin and clapped me on the shoulder. "They believe me," he said. "I'm the son. Think I should change my name?"

"I don't know much about you, Mr. de Worde," I said.

"You can call me, *Wynk.*"

"Where'd you grow up, anyway?"

"I've gone over that," said Sable." He waved a file folder.

[continued on p. 154]

fellow jimmying open your trunk. What did he get?"

"Some stories I wrote. Writers do worry. Like somebody publishing your stuff under another name. Aw, heck. They're not great stories."

"But it got you poking around in the Park Blocks."

I laughed. "Yeah, me the detective."

"How's the search going?"

"I think I hit a dead end. A guy told me he sold them to the Wild Man."

"You get a description?"

"Runs around naked."

Zapf looked off at the traffic going past. "That's new," he said, "The Wild Man coming downtown."

"You know him?"

"I know a lot of guys."

"They say he's hard to find."

"You gotta know where to look."

"Maybe I should hire you," I said.

"No need for that. I reckon he'll take good care of your stories."

"That's a joke, right?. Hey, wait a minute. Why were you following me?"

"There's been some trouble, and there might be more."

"You mean the shooting."

"I mean I'm riding shotgun on you for a spell."

"You think I'm in danger?"

"Don't worry, I'll keep an eye on ya."

The next day, Zapf appeared at my office door. He didn't notice Monica.

"Now what?" I said.

"Well, that Longfellow article you wrote. I had a chance to read it when I was in the hospital."

"How did you get a copy?"

"A friend from here sent me one. "

"Not Wynk?"

"Nah. You sure you translated the part about Sir Francis Drake right?"

"It was Jane Schoolcraft's translation. The original—if you can believe it—resembled Old Icelandic."

"I'm interested in Drake," said Zapf. "And his visit to Oregon."

"Well," I said. "If you recall your 4th-grade history—Sir Francis Drake only got as far as California. He never made it to Oregon."

"But your legend says—"

"It's a story. That's what I keep telling Caxton. It's not *history*."

Zapf was silent. "I think we'd better take a little trip to the Oregon coast. I reckon you can take another day off."

"How far is it?"

"People from Portland go for the day, then come right back. We'll take that hot VW you were driving."

Two hours later, Highway 6 opened into the town of Tillamook. My shot-gun-riding passenger had slept all the way.

I nudged him when we came to an intersection.

"Which way do I go? I asked him.

"Straight, then left, left," he said. "When you come to the Tillamook Pioneer Museum, park the car."

Zapf took me and Monica down the basement of the building. In a glass case was an exhibit on loan from two investigators: Wayne Jensen and Don Viles. It displayed their evidence for Sir Francis Drake's visit to Oregon

"Check this out," said Zapf, indicating a map. It showed Drake's mythical New Albion—the harbor he'd supposedly found for the English—superimposed on something they called Nehalem Bay.

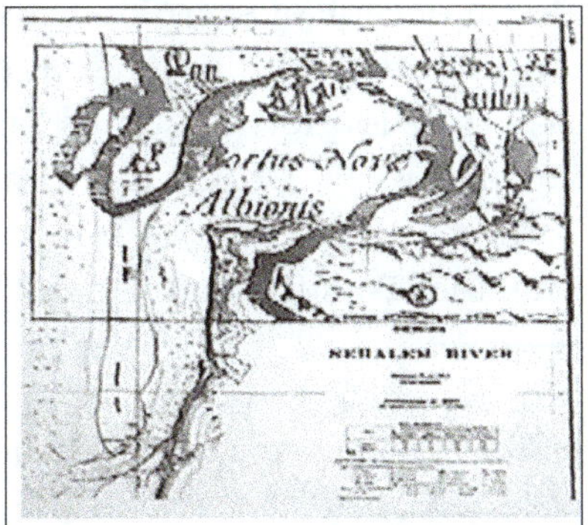

"What does that prove?" I said.

"Nehalem Bay was his harbor."

"Very iffy," I said, not convinced.

Zapf jabbed a finger at the glass cases. "How about all this?"

"These rocks with scratches they claim were survey markers—they're probably a 19th-century hoax."

"Hell you're stubborn!" said Zapf and stormed up the stairs.

Outside I found him next to the car. "I'm sorry," I said. "If you just had an expert—you might convince me."

"*Expert?* Why didn't you say so. Get in the car."

Zapf drove to a house on a residential street. A heavyset, older fellow opened the door. Zapf introduced him as Wayne Jensen. He took us into a cluttered office.

Jensen explained the puzzle which he and Don Viles had solved after a decade of searching rugged terrain and consulting aerial photos. They found the stones mark-ing a survey Drake must have ordered during his 16th-century visit.* He intended to claim this area for England. Was the claim ever filed?

———

* Wayne Jensen, "The Lost English Claim to the Northwest," in *Tales of the Neahkanie Treasure* Tillamook County Historical Society (1991).

Zapf must have sensed I was wavering. He took me back to the museum basement to show me a rock they'd shoved behind the glass case.

"Can you make out what somebody scratched on there?"

I was a little stunned. "Gosh, I said. "I probably can." I wrote out the symbols on a piece of paper for him: Sč/Ƚ.

"What's it say?" asked Zapf.

"It's just the letter-sounds of Skwch."

"Sasquatch?"

"Aw, man," I groaned. "Somebody went to a lot of trouble to set this whole thing up. The rocks, the letter to Longfellow. It's only taken 150 years to spring the trap."

"You still think it's a hoax. What about the place-names in your Nokomis legend?"

"Oh, that mountain—I forget the name. It doesn't really exist does it?"

"Get in the car," said Zapf. "We're driving north on Highway 101."

On the way, he called out the places we went through. He said he pictured it all from the air— as if in flight.

"Amazing," said Monica.

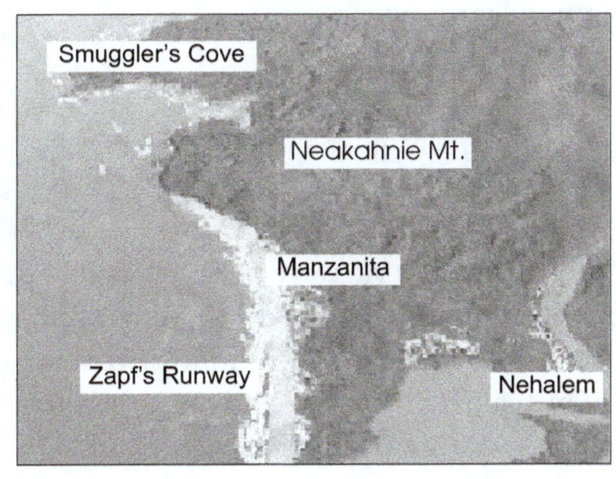

After Nehalem, I followed the signs to Manzanita, but Zapf told me to turn off before we got there. The gravel road ended in dunes.

We got out and I heard the muffled roar of the Pacific. Zapf scrambled up a path through dune grass. I followed, but had to pause at the top to take in the expanse that opened up. In both directions the wide beach stretched out deserted. The Pacific swept in like the surf in a Matthew Arnold poem.

Zapf was wrestling some brush in a hollow, throwing branches aside. Hidden there was an red airplane!

"Help me haul this baby out," he hollered. "The ranger at the State Park, lets me keep it here." Zapf pointed north to a purple rise in the distance. "There's your mountain." he said. "Come on. I'll take you on a little ride in my Cessna."

"Oh goody," said Monica.

Could I trust this fellow to actually fly an airplane? And would the rickety thing fly?

"You'll see everything" said Zapf. "Especially Smuggler's Cove."

"Is that important?" I asked.

"It is to my part of the story. Let's go. Come on." We taxied down the beach. Then suddenly we were aloft, over the little town of Manzanita. Zapf made a wide turn over a bay, then gunned the engine over the mountain. He pointed out the cove, then circled out to sea and back, coming to rest—impossibly—on a mountain ledge.

I looked out over Nehalem Bay and the Pacific. "An important place?" I said.

"Sure. Wayne thinks it's the place Drake picked out and claimed for an English harbor. But I think it was the smaller Smuggler's Cove—behind us."

"I saw too much surf for a harbor."

"In 1579, who can say?"

"Say, I notice that you've landed your plane on top of this mountain."

"It's not easy."

"How do you get down?"

"Gun the engine, tip it over the cliff."

"I think we better walk down."

"I've got another place to show you."

Monica and I struggled to keep up with spry Zapf on trails across the mountain.

Finally he stopped and hushed me. From some deep pocket he extracted a video camera and pointed into the bushes. I saw some movement in the trees. But

Zapf had already withdrawn to rewind his tape. "Look in the eyepiece. You'll see," he said. *Continued on p. 168*

Portland behind the times

**#14 Searching
for Margo**   *[continued from p. 141]*

Serial fiction by Anton Garamond

*The story so far: To get information about Margo—
who may be dead—Luke has left the baby behind
and agreed to deliver a rare coin to the Oregon Historical Society.*

Luke found his yellow Riter truck still parked in the lot. A shaggy looking character came out of the woods and stared at the vehicle. The guy looked inflated—probably he was wearing six raincoats in layers.

"This your truck?" asked the guy. He'd spotted the bullet holes that Slade had made when Luke drove off with the baby.

"My truck? No sir," Luke fibbed.

"Well the word is out on the grape-vine. People from the east side are looking for this truck."

"People?" said Luke.

"Yeah, a little greaser named Slade. He packs a gun. And his partner's a big fellow—"

"A guy with a beard, named Garbage?" said Luke. "Never heard of them." Now Luke was alarmed. Even his recent past was catching up with him. How did these hobos and thugs keep in touch? Tin-cans and a long string, maybe?

The guy fumbled at an inner pocket. Eventually he hauled out a cellular phone. "Maybe I should call the FBI," he said. "There might be a reward."

"Oh, you don't want to call them," said Luke, grinning. "You want to give me directions to the Oregon Historical Society!"

The shaggy fellow's face brightened.

"They got real nice benches outside," he said. "Take Burnside down the hill. Take a right at Burger King"

"Is it a long walk?"

"Walk? Take a Portland free bike!"

Luke noticed that the brush around the parking lot was littered with yellow bicycles."

"Use it and leave it!" said the fellow.

Luke thanked the guy, chose a bike, and soon was racing down Burnside for his first visit to downtown Portland. But he hadn't slept now for over two days. And things got strange very fast.

Past Fred Meyer's, the street turned into a plank road. It was murder riding the hard bike-seat. At Weinhardt's Brewery, saloons began lining the roadway. Luke skillfully steered his bike around horse-drawn wagons and mounds of horse manure.

Outside Erikson's Saloon a big crowd flowed out onto the wooden sidewalk. Rough men hoisted schooners of beer as Luke skidded to a stop.

"Look, it's a dandy on one of those bye-cycles!"

"Where's the Burger King?" puffed Luke.

"Beats me," said a fellow in calk boots. But the Cattle King, Peter French, and his boys just got into town. And drinks are on the house!"

None of this really surprised Luke. Back east, people pictured Portland as a kind of frontier town. He gazed at the bearded loggers, rough sailors, and cowboys in chaps as they lurched in and out of the big saloon. It was worse than he'd expected. Portland had never advanced into the 20th- century.

[continued]

Chinatown tunnel probed

**#15 Searching
for Margo**

Serial fiction by Anton Garamond

*The story so far: To gain information about Margo,
Luke is trying to deliver a coin to downtown Portland. But he finds Burnside lined with saloons, loggers, and cowboys.*

It was getting dark. Through the doors of Erikson's Saloon
Luke glimpsed a massive hall ringed by balconies. Over
the railings hung plump ladies making lewd gestures at the
crowd below. So this was night life in Portland?

Luke wound through ghostly downtown streets on his
yellow bicycle, past the big Portland Hotel ("Special rates
for families and single gentlemen"), past Terwilliger's
Blacksmith shop, past advertisements declaring "Rupture
Cured" and "Lost Manhood Restored."

Toward the river, the streets were thronged with Chinese people. They hurried past in a dizzying display of dili-
gence—all of them, workaholics.

Except one. Luke parked his bike next to a jaunty fellow leaning against a cast-iron lamppost. He wore a pigtail
hanging out the back of his derby.

"I'm confused," said Luke. "What year is it?"

"It's 1895," said the fellow. "And you need more opium!"
The guy shoved him toward a doorway.

"Hold it—" Luke began to explain by displaying Professor Overton's Chinese coin.

The fellow seized it. "Dice? Girls?"

"Listen," said Luke. "Overton told me to—"

"Overton? You want Nancy Boggs' place. Hey, I got
shortcut."

Before Luke could reply, the fellow had opened a trap-
door in the wooden sidewalk. Luke felt himself dragged

down into a dark tunnel.

"We go under Front Street," said his guide. They came out under a wharf. From upstream came the sound of a sawmill working the night shift. The guy pushed Luke into a rowboat. Luke snatched his coin back as a rope tied to the bow pulled him into the current. He made out lights ahead on a barge. The rowboat bumped to a stop. Rough

hands hauled him up the side of the vessel.

On deck, a skinny guy was playing honky-tonk piano. More plump women lounged on couches under the stars. A banner proclaimed, "Welcome to Nancy Boggs' Whiskey Scow."

A dour-looking woman approached. "Well finally, a customer," she said. "Evenin,' I'm Nancy."

"Not much business?" said Luke.

"Not since they built the Morrison Street bridge."

"Look," said Luke. "All I did back there was mention the name, *Overton*, and—"

"Overton!" she cried. "Right this way!"

Luke was thrust into Victorian stateroom. On a wide mahogany bed sprawled an enormous but gorgeous woman whose magnificent bosom rose up like the Grand Tetons. Sensing someone in the room, she cast velvety eyes on Luke. His knees nearly buckled as a wave of prurient desire washed over him.

"Who is she?" whispered Luke.

"Why, this is Mystic Margo, Overton's Hawaiian daughter. She's a volcano princess—and that'll cost you extra."

[continued on page 162]

[Zapf-3 continued from p. 142]

"I did some research on my own," Sable said. "It's all here."

"Can I look?" I said.

In lawyer's lingo, Sable told Wynk to scram. Then, once we were alone, he handed me the folder.

Right away my eye caught a reference to The Crystal Springs Home for Boys in Seattle. I showed the item to Sable. "What's this?" I said.

"That's where he grew up."

"You checked their records?"

"I did my best," sighed Sable. "Unfortunately, the place burned down in 1981."

"There must be a Director still alive who'd remember him."

"Dead," said Sable.

"De Worde must have gone to high school in Seattle."

"Actually, the foster home had its own school."

Now, Gordon Sable has hired me, off and on, for years. I thought I knew him pretty well. For example, he forbids people to take photographs of him. Just then, he had a fatigued air that didn't match the fellow I'd seen play doubles tennis. And there was something else I'd never seen before. He was lying to me.

"Okay." I said, turning back to the folder. "It says he went to college up in Bellingham."

"We've got his transcript for that. He was an English major."

"And this is his actual social security number?"

"Right."

I stood up. "Well, good work, Gordon. I've got to catch a plane to Reno. Can you pay my airfare?"

"Reno? I don't under-stand," he said.

"It's about the murder. I'm trying to clear your wife."

"Oh poor Lauren. She's worse. I've got her in Hill-crest—a private hospital. Lately she's been con-fessing to the crime. Can you imagine that?"

I told him about catching up with the supposed hit-man. "But I don't think he shot Culligan," I said. "Why would he say he was here to rough somebody up?"

Gordon looked distressed by the topic. "Poor dead Peter," he said, waving me away. "Do what you have to do," he said.

On my way to the airport I made a call to Police De-tective Trask. He owed me a favor and agreed to run Wynk's name and social security number through law enforcement files in Seattle and Bellingham.

By mid-afternoon I was in Reno renting a car. Tommy'd

Not enough hours in the day?

Busy achievers have a secret: The **26-hour Watch!**

Simply paste one of our faces on your own watch, clip off the minute hand, and you'll discover a world of *new time!*

Our hours are just shorter: 55-1/2 min-utes. The watch above points to red-7 a.m. Time to wake up and be at work by 9 o'clock, *your* time. So they say you're a little late—they'll get used to it. At 11 am, join friends for lunch—noon, their time. And when it's time to quit, a bit late (at your 5 o'clock), they'll want to know your secret. Because after midnight, <u>you're got two extra hours</u> nobody else has!

Order yours today from Zapf Inc.
Pioneer Square, PDX. OR.

told me his boss hung out at Generous Joe's. The place turned out to be some kind of graphics shop. The pasty-faced guy out front told me they could make copies inside for ten cents a page.

"Tempting," I said. "But I'm here to see Mr. Schwartz."

The guy gave me a look I didn't like, then went inside. I get a special feeling when things in a case are clustering and coming into focus. I had the feeling then.

The guy came back. With him was that greasy little shrimp, Tommy.

"You got here fast," I told him.

"That's me," he said. "Tommy the Rabbit."

They led me past some computers and a dark room to an office. Nobody was behind the desk. I spun around. The pasty-faced guy was coming at me, swinging a metal T-square. I dodged that and faced Tommy. He sneered and waved a switch-blade at my face. This would be easy, I thought. Then someone sapped me from behind. I went to my knees. When I looked back, pasty-face was hefting a metal box. It was a waxer. After it slammed into my mug, the hot liquid wax ran burning, down my neck. But I got up again. Tommy was pointing an aerosol can at me—spray fixative, right in the eyes. I was blinded and down. So they started kicking: in the gut, in the groin, in the ribs and in the head.

I must have passed out for a few minutes. My stinging eyes brought me to. I heard Tommy say he was going to wash my eyes out with something he'd found in the darkroom. I caught a whiff of benzene.

"You idiot," said a new voice. "Use olive oil. Look in

the kitchen."

I let them swab my eyes with oil. Squinting, I could make out a bald guy with a cigar in his mouth. He had my wallet open. But then everything became transformed—more clear—as if a font had changed in mid-sentence.

"So you're the big boss," I said.

"And you're a two-bit dick from Portland. You want we should play the violin while we bust your balls?"

"Murder across state lines is a Federal rap," I said.

"What's he talking about, Tommy."

"It's just Culligan, Mr. Schwartz. He got shot."

"What!" hollered his boss.

"I didn't do it," said Tommy.

"Crl," muttered Schwartz. "Pete and his big plans. How'd it happen, Tommy?"

"Culligan and me, we just talked there at the door. Then, what the J7d, I beat it—"

"Hey, I sent you to lean on somebody. Those people owe me three hundred grand."

"I'll take care of it, for sure."

"What about my casinos? My Indian casinos?" said Schwartz.

"So that's your angle," I said.

"You're an idiot," he said. "Just like these guys. Like wasted Culligan. Midgets. Dwarves." I heard Schwartz walk off, saying, "I'm surrounded by midgets, phonies, and dwarves!"

After that they worked me over some more. They were going to dump me in Lake Tahoe. But Tommy said I was an okay dude. So they loaded my battered mug in my rented car and left it outside an emergency room.

It took three days in the hospital before I could reach the phone beside my bed. The first call I made was to Detective Trask in Portland.

"How'd you do in Reno," he asked.

"Not too good," I said.

"I only found one thing on your guy, Wynk de Worde. A problem with Immigration. In May he got stopped coming off the ferry at Anacortes driving with a Canadian license."

"How far is that from Bellingham?"

"About forty miles. He produced a U.S. birth certificate. So they let him off."

"Thanks," I said. "By the way, that Tommy Lemberg. Scratch him off your list of suspects."

Then I called the airlines and made a reservation on a flight to Bellingham. The next day I discharged myself.

Bellingham is a nice town. The University campus sits next to a wooded hill. I found the English department in the Humanities building, but the one old professor who might recall de Worde from the late 1970s had recently retired.

My next stop was Alumni House on the edge of campus. But I had a hunch. Never ignore a hunch. Strether had said that Wynk worked for a time in Development. The Foundation offices were not far away. Both are names for *money* in university life.

Reaching the Old Main building involved a long climb up two flights of stairs. Tough, for an old fella like me who's been beat up. But I needed the exercise.

Inside a graduate student was manning the front desk at lunchtime. Innocently I asked for Mr. de Worde.

"Oh, he left in the Spring," she said. "You a friend of his?"

I said I was.

"Wynk—that's what everyone called him, "she said. "Wynk had great parties at his place. You know the big brick house over on Hooker? He rented the upstairs."

Hooker street turned out to be a leafy dead-end. I rang the bell of the only brick house on the block. A rough-hewn lady in a house coat answered the door. When I mentioned de Worde's name, she beamed.

"How's he doing?" she asked. "Imagine, getting a Hollywood contract. Of course I saw him in that play. Nobody knew a producer was in the audience."

"He told you all this?" I said.

She put on a pout. "Well, actually— Wynk was a little secretive. But that Reichler woman came by after he left. She told me the whole story."

"Reichler?"

"His friend. Ada Reichler. Her father owns one of the shipping docks on the waterfront. You know that big house over on Lawnford?"

My map of Bellingham told me where to go next. I found the Reichler mailbox and drove up a gravel drive lined with poplars.

At the side of the house, a gardner was on his knees, picking petals off petunias. "Ada?" he said. "She's up at their summer place in Sydney."

"North of Victoria?"

"Right. It's the last place out on the point. Say, I didn't catch your name."

But I was already back in my rented car. I caught a ferry at Anacortes, and in two hours drove off into British Columbia.

The Reichler place was a big shaggy lodge overlooking the water. A sporty Mercedes was parked in the drive. I pulled in next to it and climbed terraces to the house. A woman was stretched out on the shady porch reading a novel. She looked to be in her forties, but she was my type—slender, bright, nice smile.

"Don't get up," I said. "My name is Zapf. I'm a detective from Portland."

She had a wide mouth, and she pursed it now. "What's this about?"

"Wynk de Worde."

"That stinker," she said. "Is he in trouble?"

"He's claiming he's the lost son of a literary editor. But I think he's a fraud."

"Can I help him?" she said. The tone in her voice told me that hearing his name had brought it all back.

"Tell me about him," I said.

"He's a nice guy—sweet." Her eyes were clouding up. "But he was poor. You know, he grew up right here in Sydney. His real name is *John Galton*. His mother runs a motel, The Pines, near the airport."

"You've met his mother?"

"I thought of going over, after he left. But he did drive me past the motel once—to show me the kind of place he grew up in. I wish it had all been different. Now I feel so— So old."

"Don't say that. You're gorgeous."

She put her face in her hands. Then she looked up. "Are you a nice guy?"

"I can be," I said, and touched her hair, knowing this was preposterous

She stood up, wet her lips.

My heart beat wildly. Now I did hear violins. I took her in my arms.

(continued on p. 164]

Volcano Princess talks

#16 Searching
for Margo

[continued from p. 153]

Serial fiction by Anton Garamond

*The story so far: Luke has found downtown Port-
land, but the year is 1895. Aboard Nancy Boggs'
whiskey scow, the large woman in bed is Overton's
daughter, Mystic Margo.*

Luke felt light-headed. The woman on the stateroom bed
had merely stretched and yawned. But her mouth—
such a luscious sauciness—he yearned to devour it. A preposterous tide rose in his chest, surely it was love sluicing
over a brim. She was irresistible—and for sale! He writhed
in sweet agony. For no puny man could hope to satisfy this
supple goddess, this shushing presence, this landscape of
need. His journey, then, had come to this? He knew he
ought to kneel and confess his unworthiness.

Then he noticed a vacant look in her violet eyes. She

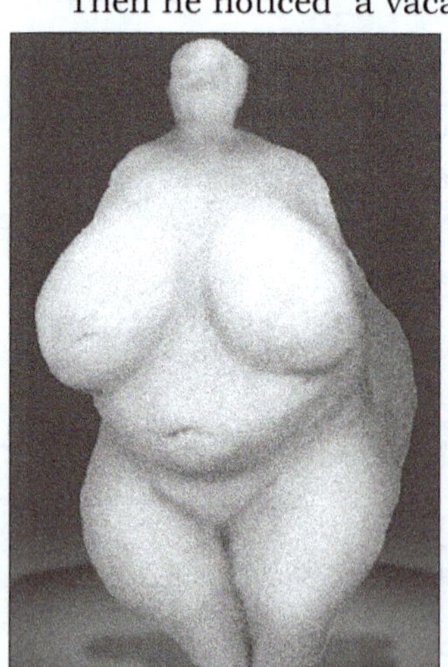

seemed to commune with some
alternate dimension. Is this
what Overton meant when he
said Margo wasn't exactly
alive?

"She's part of her father's
revenge on the men of Portland," explained Nancy Boggs.

"Men take up this chal-
lenge?"

"Hundreds. Plus all the big
local studs: Meier and Frank,
Harvey Scott and his buddy,
Pittock—even the Governor. Of
course, everybody goes limp at
the sight of Margo.

But I get paid in advance."

"Pittock?" said Luke.

"He owns *The Oregonian*, Portland's newspaper. Harvey Scott is his editor."

Just then Mystic Margo's mouth began churning out a shocking gruel of obscenities. "J7ȼıℓ ɔıψⱱ lawyers! ↄı⸀rich paper-jockeys, ıⱱ-licking ıⱱℓℓ₥₦, J7ȼıℓ mouthpieces! ȼҺȼ₰7ȼıℓ scriveners!" Abruptly, she stopped.

Nancy Boggs had squeezed the goddess's little toe. "That's PAUSE" explained Nancy. "Margo here, she's pretty smart—a walking encyclopedia. But sometimes she snaps. Now, you don't look like a lawyer. That's what usually brings on one of her spells."

"What does she have against lawyers?"

"Oh, it's connected to her father's campaign against Asa Lovejoy, a lawyer. Overton claimed Lovejoy, in 1844, cheated him out of some real-estate. Harvey Scott's a member of the bar, too"

"Why does Scott's name keep coming up?"

"Well, *The Oregonian* is his pulpit. He manipulates public opinion. He's way up in the Masonic Temple. And he's behind the Historical Society—"

"Gosh," said Luke. "That's one reason I'm here. This coin—" Luke pulled out Overton's Chinese coin. "This belongs in the Historical Society."

"I ain't seen one of those in years," said Nancy. "Overton used to hand them out, saying it's how he paid Lovejoy for some filing fee. And that would prove, he claimed, that all the land, under the city of Portland, belonged to him."

Under a whole city? thought Luke. "Overton is a old guy with a goatee?

"Nah. Overton's dead," said Nancy. "He was a shiftless eccentric from Tennessee. After murdering a man in Honolulu he showed up again in Portland with all those coins and his daughter, Margo."

Luke touched the ring on his finger. "Listen," he said, "I might be a hundred years early, but I'm supposed to deliver this ring to Margo."

"Better wait. Here's her husband."

[continued on page 166]

["Zapf-3" continued from p. 161]

In was dark by the time I arrived at The Pines Courtel, a set-up I hadn't seen for years: separate little cottages. At one end, some guys were unloading TVs, stereos, and car radios from a pick-up. When I pulled in, they dropped out of sight. Somebody here fenced stolen goods. The office—it said VACANCY—was attached to a run-down bungalow.

The door was locked. I knocked. Inside I heard the creak of bedsprings and shuffling feet. An old man opened the door. His face was bruised and he moved like he was in pain.

"Is Mrs. Galton here?" I asked.

"I'm Mr. Galton," he rasped. "A room'll cost you thirty-five dollars."

I handed him two twenties. His hand shook when he took them. "I ain't got change," he said.

"Give it to your boy," I said.

"He ain't no boy. And he run off, the little piece of ш."

Then an older woman in a nightgown appeared from a back room. "I'll take that money," she said.

The old guy crumpled the bills in his fist, but she pried it open.

"He'll just spend it on cheap wine," she said and told the old guy to go back to bed. When she saw it was American money, she asked where I was from.

"Oregon," I said.

"What brings you up here?"

"A man named Peter Culligan was shot to death two weeks ago in Portland."

"Aw. I thought he was in Reno," she sighed. "That old

dumb bunny. So Pete is really dead?"

"You knew Culligan?"

"He had a room here for a while in the Spring. Who shot him?"

"Maybe you can tell me."

"You're from the police, aren't you? It wasn't John! Not my boy."

"He might have been involved."

She winced. "I knew he was headed for trouble," she said. "He came back after being gone for years. Then, before he left, he punched his father."

"Do you have a picture of your son? There might be some mistake here."

From a drawer she brought out a snap-shot someone had taken of Wynk de Worde doing the weather on TV. "He'd made a name for himself," she said. "Just like he said."

"Said what?"

"When he was little. He used to say he was a prince, or an emperor. That gypsies had stolen him. Someday he was going to rightfully claim his kingdom."

"Right now," I said, "he's claiming to be someone else's son."

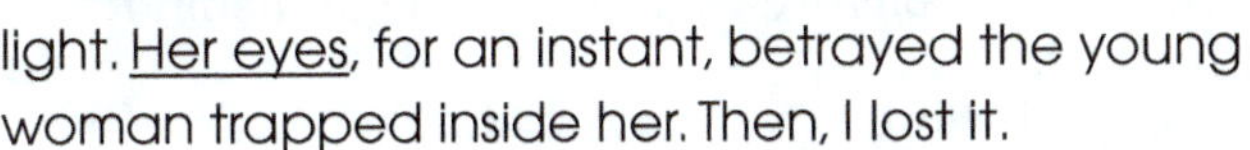

"Wynk ran off with Culligan. That Reno crook. I'm glad he's dead."

It was late. I said goodnight and stayed the night in the cottage I'd paid for. The place smelled of booze, sweat, and bad karma.

In the morning I had a chance to see Mrs. Galton outside in good light. Her eyes, for an instant, betrayed the young woman trapped inside her. Then, I lost it.

City fathers rooked settler

**#17 Searching
   for Margo**    [continued from p. 163]

Serial fiction by Anton Garamond

*The story so far: Luke has found someone named
Margo, but the year is 1895, and she's a large god-
dess-like creature on a pleasure barge.*

Nancy Boggs and Luke glanced the other way as the
skinny piano player barged in and made an amorous
dive. Velvet-eyed Margo cushioned his landing with her
ample bosom.

"That's Ludwig," said Nancy. "He's quite a kisser."

The ring on Luke's finger felt hot. He'd promised to deliver it to someone named Margo. But was this the right
person? The right century?

"Let me get this straight," he said to Nancy, the
Madam. "Margo's father owned the real-estate under the
city of Portland?"

"In 1844; just a square mile of timber."

"But a lawyer, Lovejoy, cheated him."

"And Pettygrove, too. Margo's father sold him a coin-
trick."

"Remind me who Pettygrove was."

From behind them came the horrid sound of smooching
in bed.

"Gosh, this was all before my time," said Nancy. "When
Overton didn't come back from the Sandwich Islands, Pettygrove built up the town himself."

"But he did come back." said Luke.

"As an old man, a couple years ago, with his daughter.
Instead of his timber, he found a city. Lovejoy and Pettygrove were dead."

Luke tried not to picture what was going on behind
them on the bed.

"And nobody believed Overton," said Luke.

"Would you believe a guy who spent his time calculating the mass of Mt. Hood?"

Just then a shrill whistle sounded. The piano player, emerged—as if shot from a soft cannon—and hollered, "It's a *raid!*"

"You better make a get-away," advised Nancy.

Luke stood in the doorway. Outside, women were shrieking. "Hey," said Luke. "Tell me where to find that guy who edits *The Oregonian*, Harvey Scott—and his Historical Society."

"This time of night?" said Nancy. "Try the New Market Theater. Ground floor. It's a poker game."

Somebody was yanking Luke out the door.

"Listen, Harvey's a sweet old coot!" she yelled. "He's starting a festival in honor of my girls and my rose garden. It's up on the hill, high above the city!"

Ludwig, the piano player, finally pulled Luke toward the rail. On deck, police in Keystone-Cops outfits gripped plump women about their midriffs.

"Jump!" cried Margo's husband. They landed in a rowboat. Ludwig began rowing furiously. Behind them, shouts sounded from a boat pursuing them.

A dark wharf loomed overhead. Luke gripped a ladder and scrambled up.

Library of Congress

"Run!" hollered Ludwig from below. "Don't worry about me. It's that coin they're after. They're saying some Chinaman tipped them off!"

Luke dashed across Front Street to the Skidmore Fountain. A gang of club swinging police was right on his tail.

[continued on page 170]

["Editor-4" continued from p. 149]

"What was that? I asked.

"The Wild Man." said Zapf.

"Doesn't he hang out in Portland?"

"He travels fast."

"The guy with my manuscripts?"

"Jeez," said Zapf. "Here we are on sacred Neahkahnie Mountain, catching Big Foot on tape—and all you think about are your own crummy stories."

"Big Foot has my stories?"

"Listen, what's our situation? What's our latitude?"

"Beats me," I said.

"Okay," said Zapf. Let's take a break. Have dinner. Then, once it gets dark, I'll take you on another ride."

Monica and I hiked down and met Zapf at a pretty good restaurant in Manzanita. The menu said that payment in the form of a Cuban cigar merits a free meal. Zapf graciously took the check and pulled out a beaten-up cigar.

His Cessna was parked out on the dark beach. We got in, he took off and headed out to sea. Then Zapf made a sharp turn back to land. "<u>Hold on!</u>"

Banking sharply over the lights of Manzanita, Zapf dipped dangerously low over mountain treetops. I could make out a greenish circular glow in the woods below.

"Not many people in this world," said Zapf, "have seen that sight— that's for sure."

Over beers at a tavern in town, I confessed that the glow I'd glimpsed in the woods had looked familiar.

Zapf pulled out a photo and slapped it down. "Is that what you saw?"

"Yeah, *weird*," said Monica, leaning over the photo.

"Now," said Zapf, "on foot, you can see faint phosphorescence in those trees. I've taken soil samples. A black layer I sent to the Radiocarbon Lab at UC Riverside. It was charcoal, 14,000 years old. An isotope of Carbon 14 makes it glow."

"I get it," said Monica.

"You think a meteor burned that circular pattern?" I asked Zapf.

"Nah. It must have been a structure. Big timber uprights. Somebody burned it down. Now look at this."

Zapf laid a transparency on top of the photo, then peeled it off.

The over-lay was a Stonehenge image from his crazy Sylvia Plath article.

"We aren't going to print that Plath article." I said. "We'll get sued."

"Aw, I was just havin' fun." On a little map he drew a razor-straight line. "That's latitude 45

degrees 43 minutes North." [continued on p. 174]

Oregonian editor a villain

#18 Searching for Margo  *[continued from p. 167]*

Serial fiction by Anton Garamond

The story so far: The Margo Luke finds in 1895 is the wrong one. Now, trying to locate Harvey Scott, editor of The Oregonian, he's being pursued by the Portland police

Right across from the Skidmore Fountain, Luke spotted the New Market Theater. A side door was open. Inside it was dark and smelled of rotten fruit. A lamp burned in a far corner of the warehouse.

Luke crept closer. A circle of overweight gentlemen in white shirts and suspenders sat on bags of potatoes playing cards.

"It's your deal, Harvey," said one.

A sour-looking man with a walrus mustache glared into space. "Foreign scum!" he declared. "Labor unions! Damned free public education!"

"Settle down, ante-up," said another.

"And the air in this town, this smoky haze!"

"It's just another forest fire."

"Well then, destroy the timber!" roared the old man. "Corn and wheat are more

City of Portland (OR) Archives, A2004-002.7687

to man than the finest trees!"

Luke chose this moment to approach the group. "Mr. Harvey Scott?"

A circle of shrewd, cold eyes examined the newcomer. "This is a private game," said one man. "Unless you got twenty dollars."

"Actually—" said Luke, holding up Overton's Chinese coin. "This is all I got."

"Where'd you get that?" said Scott.

"It's for your Historical Society," explained Luke. "But I'm having this problem with time, you know? Exactly what year it is."

"He's an opium eater," said one man.

"I'll give you fifty dollars for that coin," said Scott. "I'm collecting them. They're dangerous."

"So you know the real story, then," said Luke. "About Overton being cheated by Lovejoy and Pettygrove."

"The real story," declared Scott, "is that Overton was paid 25 cents plus goods and supplies for his land. And those other two flipped a penny! A coin minted in the United States of America!"

"Harvey ought to know the real story,"

huffed one man. "He wrote it!"

There came the sound of a door busting open. The cops were here.

"Get that coin and throw him out," snarled Scott. "Our deeds to the city are worthless if this goes to court!"

The Keystone Cops leapt over piles of cabbages. "There he is!" they hollered.

Luke vaulted over the poker table and dashed for an exit. Outside he sprinted a block to Chinatown. There was his yellow bicycle where he'd left it.

Behind him, he heard the clang of a horse-drawn fire engine. He ducked into a doorway and let it thunder past. It was loaded with hollering police.

Luke pedaled to Burnside and headed west through mud, then over planks, uphill. Behind him that fire en-

Library of Congress

fire-engine clanged—louder, its load of young cops scared *ʊ̃ks* as the sergeant gave the order to load shells into their new Colt revolvers.   *[continued on p. 200]*

[continued from p. 169]

Sitting there—in a small-town tavern, drinking good micro-brew ale after a day of vigorous exercise—I felt

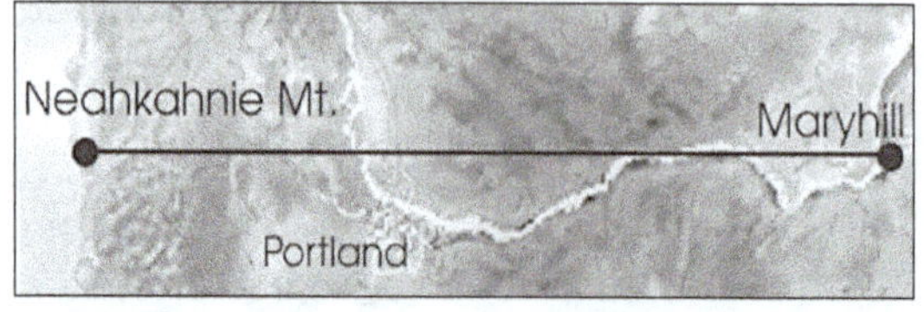

unpleasantly light-headed. I looked down at Zapf's map, at the line linking two sites, one hundred fifty miles apart.

Zapf, in his goofy Gabby Hayes outfit, had the intense look of a madman.

"I don't get it," I said. "That guy built his replica of Stonehenge in the 1920s?"

"1929," said Zapf.

"And your charcoal samples—"

Monica said, "Don't you remember your own Sasquatch Legend?"

"Hey—the overweight guy in the legend," said Zapf. "He brings out the deer-skin map? A timber circle to predict sunrise, moonset?

> Further eastward they had fashioned
> Such a temple by a river.
> And the two now marked the mid-line
> Of the Empire they had conquered."

Zapf was reciting from memory.

"It's coming back," I said. "I haven't really looked at that piece recently."

"Okay," said Zapf. "How about this: Sam Hill, the Stonehenge guy, had an aviator friend, a veteran of World War I. He flew his biplane up and down the Columbia Gorge in the 1920s. A few times the winds kept him aloft after dark, and he spotted the same green circular pattern that I showed you—but his was along the

Columbia, south of Goldendale."

"Goldendale. That's a town?"

"Where I was born, " said Zapf.

"So Hill picked his location—"

"He built *precisely* on top of an ancient site. Hill's workmen said the footings for his concrete uprights were easy to place because they were marked by charcoal in the soil."

"Okay," I sighed. "The glow I saw in the trees is at the same latitude as Sam Hill's replica of Stonehenge."

"*Exactly.* Oh, maybe it's off a couple minutes of a degree." Zapf's face was flushed with excitement.

I strained to imagine two timber Stonehenges erected hundreds of miles apart. I finally managed to say: "This was a long time ago—"

"End of the last ice-age," said Zapf. "Not bad surveyors, huh? You old buddy, *you!*"

Zapf gripped my arm as if he were greeting a long lost friend. I felt repulsed by

by his touch.

Over the bar, the neon logos blurred and tipped sideways. What was I doing here? Had I walked the earth merely to come to this: speculating about some American Stonehenge?

The beer had an aftertaste—drugged?

Zapf was mouthing words, something about my Longfellow manuscript: "...and only because you found that manuscript. Why it's got to be Fate at work. So I said to myself..."

My head was hot, but I felt a chill. I'd shown such promise when I was younger. And my concerns as a writer, teacher, and scholar were grand: peace and justice, racial equality, women's liberation, and end to the fascist merging of big business and government. Everyone, in those days, assumed one was put on earth to care for his or her corner of the world.

© Lisa McDonald. Image from BigStockPhoto.com

Just now, what I couldn't understand is why Zapf had dragged me into his looney obsessions. Flying me around in his airplane. Hauling us to museums.

"Maybe he's gay," said Monica.

"So your mother," Zapf was saying. "Evidently she grew up here in the Pacific Northwest?"

That surprised me. "I suppose," I said. "She was born and raised in Tacoma. What's the point?"

"We gotta be about the same age. Don't you think?"

I shook my head. "I doubt it."

Zapf's eyes were drilling into mine. "I've got a new theory," he said. "But you gotta read my Fourth Report." He handed me a sheaf of pages.

"But I didn't finish the Third."

"You can go <u>back to page 142</u>."

"Hey, this is handwritten—I think."

Zapf's Fourth Report

At the Victoria airport I caught a flight back to Portland. On the way, I went over my notes about the case. De Worde must have had help putting together his phony childhood history. Who could have found a Foster home in Seattle that had burned to the ground with all its records? On the ground in Portland I put in a call to Hillcrest, the hospital where Sable had stashed his wife. They said it would be impossible to speak with Mrs. Sable—because her husband had taken her home. My Datsun was still in the lot where I'd left it on the way to Reno.

Twenty minutes later I pulled into Sable's driveway. Through the hedge I caught a quick glimpse of Caxton's wife loading a suitcase into her car. Wynk

The Wynk de Worde Line

by
Richard Austin
New York &
San Francisco

wasn't in sight. In Victoria his mother had told me he'd run off with Pete Culligan. That meant Culligan knew the secret of Wynk's Canadian identity. There it was: De Worde's motive for murder. And now he'd nearly convinced Caxton that he was his long-lost son—his heir. Okay, this guy Wynk was a self-promoting asshole. But a murderer? To make sure, I had to question Sable's wife. She had to have seen the shooting.

I walked over to say hello to Margo.

"Oh," she said. "We heard you were hospitalized—somewhere."

"I'm okay. Have you seen what's-her-name, Sable's wife?"

"Loren? The poor dear." Margo glanced over at her neighbor's house. "Gordon brought her home—can believe it? She's always been more than he can handle."

"Old guy, young wife, huh?"

"You mean, old guy, show-girl. Not to put too fine a point on it."

"That's a side to Gordon I never understood. Where'd he find her?"

"Reno. A couple years ago. This spring she ran off. He located her hanging around with some man she used to know there. I heard she ran up some big gambling debts."

I was stunned for a moment. They weren't after Caxton. The mob in Reno had sent Tommy out to lean on *Sable* for his wife's gambling debts. How much did Schwartz say? Three hundred grand. And Culligan. Was the dead guy her old friend in Reno?

"Have you talked to her," I asked. "Since the shooting?"

"Gordon won't let anyone near her. But she's pretty resilient. I think she'll mend."

I looked in the trunk of the BMW she was loading. "Where's your hot little VW?"

"I loaned it to Strether. He's taken to racing around these narrow roads. I think I saw a girl with him. What did we used to call that? Road-tripping."

"You're off on a trip yourself."

"Oh, I need a break."

I nodded, wished her well, and went over to Sable's place. I found him inside working on a fifth of scotch.

"Have a drink," he said glumly.

"Sure," I said. "How's Loren?"

He glanced up and said, "I know you made a call to the hospital."

I gave him a hard look. "Do you pay these people to keep you informed?"

"I learned that from you."

Gordon Sable looked beat, as if he'd lost a big tennis match. Now he was desperate to find the exit.

From the next room sounded a banging thud. It was his wife. Loren came in wearing a thigh-length night-gown, her hair was tangled, and her pupils were dilated.

"Get back to bed," hissed Sable.

Her eyes drifted to me. "We've got company," she said—and smiled.

"Hello," I said. "I'd like to talk."

"Me too. I gotta talk to somebody."

Sable stood up. "Back to bed, Loren."

"I feel so bad," she said. "I killed Peter. And now I'm going to die."

"Tell me about the shooting?" I said. "Was Wynk there?"

"There was a party, at Bill's house."

"Shut up, Loren," said Sable."

"Everybody was out on the deck. And this little guy—I

used to see him around in Reno—rang the bell at our place, but he wanted Peter, so I took him over to Bill's."

From her description, I recognized Tommy. "This little guy," I said. "Did he have a gun?"

"I Had The Gun," stated Loren. She was reciting. "Back to bed!" hollered Sable. He was opening a closet.

"Peter answered the door at Bill's. He knew the little guy. They talked for a while. Then the guy left, so I stepped inside. I like parties."

"Loren!" Sable was yelling.

"Peter had been cleaning up in the living room. He sees me. He takes me in his arms the way he used to. People are right outside on the deck, but the drapes are shut. And I'm so hungry for him. He pulls me down on thecouch and I'm kissing him all over, and he knows this thing I like him to do—"

© Mehmet Alci. Image from BigStockPhoto.com

Abruptly Loren stopped.

Behind me a I heard the bolt of a rifle slide a cartridge into the chamber. It was Sable. He was pointing a Remington 770 .30-06 with a scope at my throat.

"Say what happened next," Sable told his wife.

"Peter, the rude, Dirty Man—" Loren searched the ceiling for the words. "He tried to tear my clothes off! So I shot him." She smiled like a girl competing in a spelling bee.

"Okay, Zapf," snarled Sable. "You satisfied? Now get the hell out of here. Get out!"

I edged toward the door. "Easy, Gordon," I said. Loren made some motion that flicked Sable's eyes away for an instant. That was my chance. I dove straight at him, gripping the barrel of the rifle as I turned over in the air. I landed on my feet in front of him, the rifle in my hands.

When I swept his feet out from under him, he gave me an astonished look. Then he fell—splat—on his face.

Loren smiled at me. "Cool," she said.

Putting my foot on Sable's neck, I pulled back the bolt and ejected the cartridge. Then I gave Loren a bright look. "You were saying?" I asked.

"About Peter?"

"Do you remember shooting him?"

"I must have done it."

"You two were alone."

"Well, Gordon came in. He saw us on the couch and told me to get up. And then—"

Loren's face nearly looked illumined. "I didn't shoot Peter. *Gordon did.*"

From the floor Sable said, "Don't believe her. She's hallucinating."

"Peter's neck—" said Loren. "It sort of exploded. Red blood spattered on the couch.

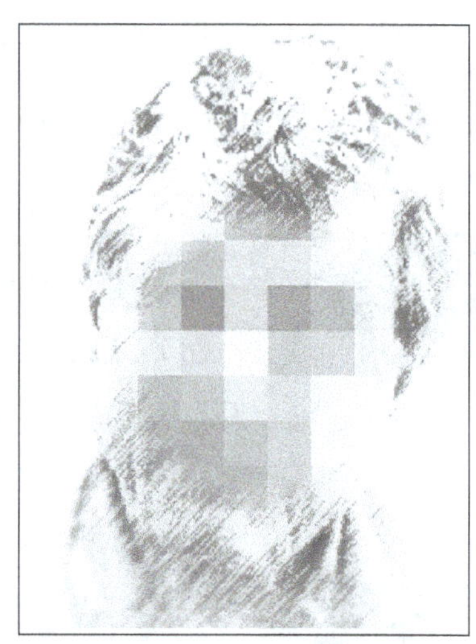

Gordon Sable

Small Press Business Manager of the Year, 2001
The American Quarterly Review
Presented by AASLP:
American Association of Small and Literary Presses

(Permission not granted to use the original image.)

Then Gordon gave me the gun. It was so heavy. 'Look what you did,' he told me. I stood there alone with poor Peter. Did I say anything? Did I scream? I don't remember."

Behind me, someone now knocked at the door.

"Go away," I called.

Loren's eyes were full of tears. "I didn't kill him," she said. It looked as if this was news to her.

"Yoo hoo?" A short woman wearing glasses looked in the door.

"Hey, we're busy in here," I told her.

Spotting Sable face down on the floor, she barged in. "Ah-ha! Now I found you!" she brightly announced.

"Please," I said. "This is very delicate moment."

The woman ignored me. She squatted down and peered at Sable's squashed face. "You can't fire me," she declared. "I've been this magazine's designer, proofreader, rights-and-permissions person—you name it—for twenty-five years. Gordon, it's me. Maddy Goedieff!"

"I didn't shoot you," said Sable.

"I know," she said. "It was Wynk."

"Wynk shot someone?" I said.

"No, no," said Maddy. "I'm using a metaphor. Wynk fired everybody. He blew the budget."

Loren sniffed and said, "What a mean thing to do."

Maddy stood up. "Why, Loren. It's good to see you. We missed you so."

"Really?"

"Oh, you poor dear." Maddy went over to hug Sable's wife.

"Say," I said, shifting my weight on Sable's neck and hefting the Remington 770 .30-06 with a 40 mm scope. "Maybe you two could step into the next room?"

"Come on, Loren," said Maddy. "We'll both have a good cry. Then we'll fix the fine mess these men have made."

When they were gone, I took my boot off Sable's neck and let him up. He eased himself into a chair and put his face in his hands. There was a phone on the end table. I called Detective Trask and told him to come right over."

I looked at Sable. "Why did you kill him?" I said.

Gordon stared straight ahead. "I couldn't stand it anymore." Then the attorney in him took a breath and let it out slowly. "I have the right to remain silent," he stated.

"Aw, Gordon. Tell me anyway." I sat down, ready for a long speech.

"What the hell," said Gordon. "That afternoon, I was out on Bill's deck with the others. I spotted Tommy Lemberg coming over from my place with Loren. I recognized him as a little thug who'd threatened me in Reno. So I went over and got my pistol. But he'd left by the time I barged in on Loren and Culligan. You heard what she said. The barnyard sex they both enjoyed. Pigs in rut. I'd forbidden her to be alone with him. But they found ways to meet."

"Your wife," I said. "She knew Culligan from—"

"From Reno. She went there in the spring to divorce me. But she ran into Culligan, a hood she knew from— Oh, from *before*."

I watched Sable brush away memories of romancing a show-girl.

"He saw she had money now," Sable went on. "And he helped her gamble it away. It all went to a Casino owner named Murray Schwartz. I got to Reno in April to bring her home. By then she owed them $300,000. Back in Portland, we lived a twisted life as strangers. I hated her. And I was in debt to a mobster."

"So Schwartz sent Culligan out here to collect his money?"

"No," said Sable. "Schwartz had nothing to do with it. Culligan showed up in May with a plan of his own. He'd seen the notice Bill sent to newspapers around the country about a missing heir. Recently he'd hooked up with a fellow in Canada about the right age and appearance. Culligan was certain this Canadian could convince Bill he was his missing son. Once they got access to the Caxton assets, there'd be enough money for everyone— me included. But there were legal details that Culligan couldn't fathom. So he came to me for help. He knew I was desperate for money.

"And this fellow from Canada?"

"John Galton," said Gordon. "He'd had some Canadian TV experience. In May he had a part in a play up in Bellingham under the name *Wynk de Worde.* I went up to see it and was impressed. So I introduced myself as a Hollywood producer, flew him down here to Portland, and laid out

a real-life part for him to play

"The idea of being the son of someone else—I gathered his father was a no-good drunk—sparked something in him. In a day or two he called to say he'd do it. I began assembling his fictitious biography. That foster home in Seattle that burned down—a stroke of genius, don't you think?"

"So how did Galton know 'Caxton' was the father's name?"

"He'd seen the newspaper ad."

"So he could have sent for the birth certificate?"

"He asked to do that himself."

I recalled Doc Stone, sitting among his Egyptian artifacts, comparing me to a previous visitor—Wynk must have been there in May. "But wait," I said. "Bill is your old buddy. How much were you going to siphon out of his assets?"

"Ah," sighed Gordon. "Bill would've paid anything to believe he had son. Now, I handle his finances. If a half million dollars was missing when I filed his next tax return, he'd write it off to losses in the stock market. Of course, I was desperate. Culligan was showing me a way to pay a $300,000 debt."

"But you tried to pin the murder on your wife!"

Sable made a sickly grin. At the edges it drained into madness. "She deserved it," he said. "She and Culligan. They both deserved it." ■

[for Editor's Column Part V see p. 192]

The Future of the Moon:

Vulcanism and Seismic Transformations of a Familiar Face

a Zolar Zapf *Guide*

The appearance of the moon, as we see it from earth, has not changed a great deal in the last 3.1 billion years. Before that, thin and repeated flows of lava filled basins to form the dark seas— or maria. But the core is still molten. Astronauts of the Apollo missions detected radon gas along fault-lines. They set charges to map the moon's interior. In the process, they may have started something.

Suppressed footage circulated privately

The camera which inadvertently caught this event was ready to record the rover's appearance on the other side of Tracy's Rock. Of course, when the Apollo 17 crew deployed their seismic charge, they didn't expect to take the face off a lunar mountain. (This footage, by the way, is not available at the NASA website.)

Over the last thirty years, seismic instruments left at this and other sites have sent back data of moonquakes whose intensity is increasing. Eventually these will open vents to the deep molten core. Landslides and fresh flows of lava over the lunar surface will inevitably transform the surface—even to the naked eye.

Now, what we see with the naked eye seems to shift from one observer to the next. People taught as children that there is a Man in the Moon probably pick out a few dark features and project this rather simplistic face:

The most ancient image that appears on the moon's face is the rabbit or hare.

This hare for the Great Mother goes back to the neolithic era. In the middle east, she was Astarte. In the west, she became Easter—hence, the Easter Bunny.

Some can make out her face in the mode of Kali the Destroyer: who ate men like air.

One of the more complex images seen on the moon's face is circulated by a group with access to a photograph

of Sylvia Plath taken on the coast of Ireland. They claim that since the early 1960s, this image has shoved aside the so-called Man in the Moon and replaced it with one that coincides with contemporary feminist lunar associations.

Any number of female images might get imposed on these features. Of course, that bulbous lunar schnozz poses a problem. By chance, it's just this region on the lunar surface whose fault-lines and seismic activity promise the earliest transformations.

Consider the consequences of lunar landslides and massive flows of lava to that nose's contour.

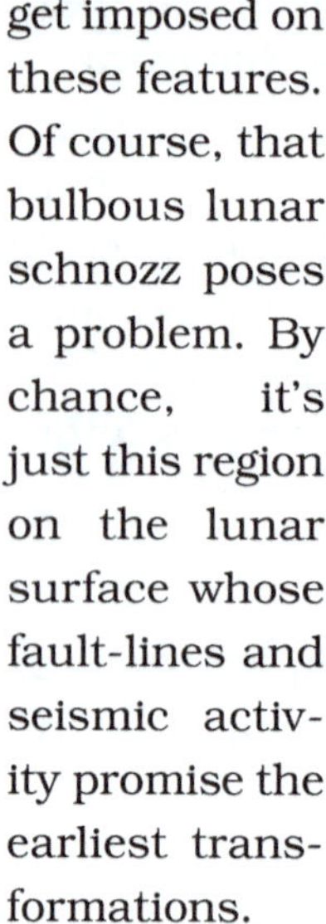

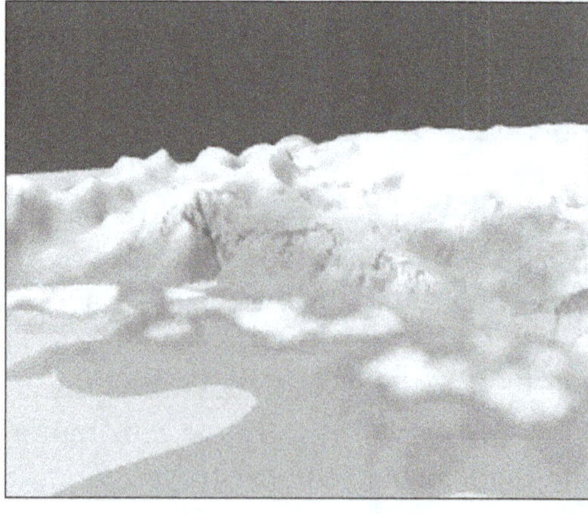

And recall that the faces humans project onto lunar features will have to map themselves onto new and slightly unfamiliar light and dark regions. It will especially be the flows of cooling and reflective—therefore light-gray—lava that are likely to transform the moon's

appearance, as seen by the naked eye.

Some viewers have already reported sighting a woman's face that resembles the one in the following demonstration. Notice how computer models predict that massive changes in the lunar surface begin with that sensitive area of Luna's nose. ∎

The Editor's Column Part IV

Before we'd landed for beers in Manzanita, Zapf had made a wide turn over the ocean, set the flaps, and descended. He steered along a line of surf that glittered in the moonlight.

"Landing a small aircraft on a wide beach at sea level—" he'd said. "It's easy—even at night."

He was right. The landing gear touched down in a silky spray of sand, and we circled to a stop. I offered to help push the Cessna back into the dunes, but he said he'd probably fly back tonight to Portland. In any case, he had a call to make in Manzanita.

"You want me to drive Margo's VW back to Portland by myself?" I asked.

"Just follow Highway 26. It'll take you right downtown."

"You're riding shotgun, remember? My life is in danger?"

"Aw, I was fibbing."

"Nobody fibs about that."

"Well, I wanted you to see the wild man.

"It was worth it," said Monica.

"And you were so concerned about your lost manuscripts—" said Zapf.

"This whole thing is preposterous," I declared. "For one thing, how could a naked man get to here from Portland in a couple hours? He'd need a—"

"Fast on his feet," said Zapf.

I glanced at Zapf's airplane. "How close have you gotten to him?" I said.

"Damn close."

"Can he talk?"

"Not much. I reckon he's pretty intelligent. Hey, let's drink beer."

Monica and I got back to Portland past midnight and parked in Caxton's driveway. From far down the slope came the faint roar of late traffic on the Interstate. On the far side of the river, a pair of locomotives hauled and hooted through the purple night.

The house was dark, except for a faint glow in a basement window. My key got us in—interlopers in the antechambers of indeterminacy.

In my room we found a message from my father's nursing home in Minneapolis. It was 3 a.m. there. I'd call in the morning.

Propped up in bed, Monica and I read through Zapf's latest *Report* by the light of a table lamp, its base a porcelain maze of Balinese arabesques. Learning that Wynk was actually a Canadian con-man named John Galton—whose ragtag family had ties to the underworld—sickened me a little, but it didn't surprise me. I read aloud about Sable's plot—hiring Wynk to get hold of Bill's assets.

"Wynk was in it for money from the mob?" said Monica.

"You think there's more to it?"

"There's gotta be more."

"Hey, listen to this," I said and read aloud about Loren Sable's tawdry sexual history, and the lurid details of Sable shooting Peter Culligan. Something shoved these desperate characters off at a distance where they clashed darkly against a bright source of light like cardboard silhouettes jointed at the shoulders and hips by rivets, and moved on sticks directed by unseen hands.

"Zapf's view is interesting, don't you think?" she said

"He's a man of honor," I said. "But he's obviously fascinated."

Okay," she said. "Attracted but also repelled. What if that's essential to a detective's character—and to his art?

"We're not like that, are we?" I said.

Monica was falling asleep. I saw now that I circled only the margins of these sordid affairs. For that distance I was grateful. Aloof from such events, I knew that I'd stepped only into the shallows of corruption, and surely within reach was a fresh streamlet, an imagined tributary of this conceit, in whose cleansing waters I could— Thinking this garbage, I too, must have dozed off.

The next morning, Monica had made coffee. But the kitchen was deserted. No one sat on the deck. The long corridor of magazine offices stretched out its locked, silent doors. In this place, formerly bustling with activity, I found myself utterly alone.

At my own office desk, I woke up the computer. A new

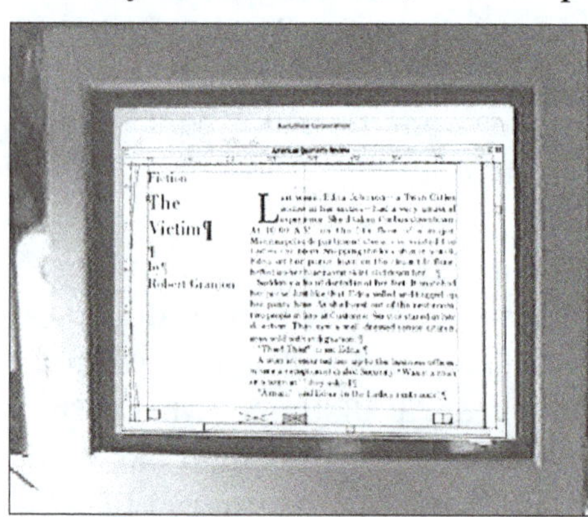

page, set up in the Magazine's layout, shimmered into view. Seeing it, I choked on hot coffee, careful not to spew onto the keyboard.

On the screen was the text of one of my stolen Minneapolis stories, ascribed to one "Robert Granjon!" The guy had evidently plagiarized my work. But how did it get accepted so fast at this magazine without going through my editorial hands?

Taped to the telephone was the number of Kurtzview's Technical Support Services. I punched it in and heard a hoarse voice say, "Yes?"

"I don't know if you can help me," I said, "but there's something peculiar on my screen. Of course, plagiarism isn't a federal offense—"

"Oh, Strether. It's you."

"Who is this?"

"Technical Support."

"Where are you, Calcutta?"

"I'm in the basement."

"Wait a minute. You're *The Guy in the Basement?*" Wynk had referred to this fellow. I'd never met him.

"Maybe it's time we had a little talk," he said. "Better come down here."

"The basement? How do I get there?"

"The stairs. Across from Maddy's office."

"They're blocked off," I said.

"Not if you've got the key."

"What key?"

"It's hidden behind the light switch. But you gotta <u>take the short-cut</u>."

I made my way down four flights of dingy stairs, but then turned back when I heard a phone ringing.

The desk phone was still ringing when I snatched the receiver and huffed, "Yes?"

"Sorry to disturb you. This is Samantha Spink. Are you asleep?"

"Not exactly," I said, thinking no one but me would have heard this phone ringing from deep in a basement. "It's about my dad, isn't it?"

"I'm sorry to say it is."

I felt a door slam in my chest. "How long—" I said, searching for the word, "—has he been *gone?*"

"You've seen the news then?"

I tried to think. "News?"

"I was up late," said Miss Spink, "writing a report. And there he was, on CNN! I've tried to reach you for days."

And then I heard her face contort as she stifled an appalling fit of laughter.

"*You* were the one calling me," I hissed into the phone. "And you think this is funny?"

"Oh, I'm sure they'll catch him and bring him back. But the idea of him just taking off— It makes me laugh."

"What are you talking about?"

"Your father. He drove off in a motorized wheelchair. He'd done something to the engine. CNN said a trucker clocked him going 57 miles per hour on the North Dakota Interstate. Turn on your TV."

Monica appeared. "Your dad isn't dead," she said.

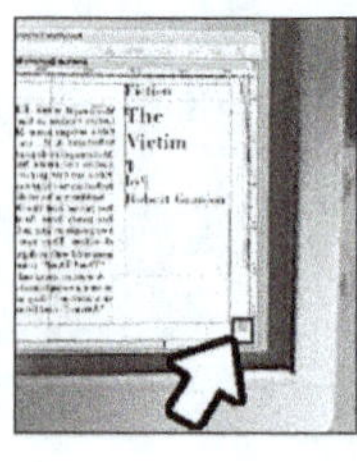

I hung up on Miss Spink and we poked around Caxton's house for the television. There wasn't one. But I recalled seeing, at one corner of my computer monitor, a little button labeled, "News."

Back in my office I dared to click it.

KurtzView 19.01.2
KurtzView Corporation
http://www.KurtzVie
Stop
Back
Forward
RePost
Home
Porn
Breaking News
Home Delivery
Kurtz News Times
Any relation to persons living or dead is based on pure coincidence and will not constitute any basis for legal action against Klurtzview, its heirs, or corporate managers.

Wheelchair Speedster Sets New Record

Clocked at 57 mph on a N.D.Highway. Scroll down for the full story.

Portland Scientist Predicts Earthquake, Eruptions, Soon

Schools in Crisis: Déjà Vu?

Wildman Captured in Oregon

Wynk DeWord's Video Report->

A creature resembling a human being was seized last weekend in the coast range. One member of the search team described a wild pursuit through tree-tops. The leader of the group, scholar and adventurer Zolar Zapf, claims that he's been observing the wildman for several years. "The time was ripe to announce my find," he said.

Zapf has led a number of expeditions in search of the fabled Sasquatch of the NW. But this was the first time he was during the interview that he surprised onlookers by howling at the moon invoking the name, "Luna."

Jeez! That was no help. I couldn't scroll down to read about the Wheelchair Speedster in North Dakota. My god, my father was actually out there?

I punched in the number again for The Guy in the Basement.

"You again?" said a nerdy voice. "I thought you was coming down here."

"I got down," I said. "But there was a phone call. Listen, I need help."

"You heard an upstairs phone ringing all the way from the basement?"

I explained my difficulty with the KurtzView Browser."

"It's a piece of shit," he said. "I seen some of the code."

"Just tell me how to get the *News*."

"Do you know all I gotta do down here? Since your fancy friends ran off?"

"I'm sure you're a hard worker."

"Well it's a pain in the ass."

"Please—" I said.

"Now I gotta design the layouts, choose articles, compose the music, change the name of the magazine…"

"You're kidding. We had a dozen people up here doing those jobs."

"Hey, get down here and learn how to get the *News*."

"I'll wait here," said Monica.

"Down all those stairs?" I asked.

"Aw, it's fun. Take <u>this other short cut</u>."

[continued on p. 203]

Fed. Agents corner truck

#19 Searching
for Margo

[continued from p. 173]

Serial fiction by Anton Garamond

The story so far: On a bike, Luke pedals west on Burnside to escape the Portland police, the Fire Department, and the year 1895. But he's failed to deliver the coin.

The thud of tiring horses and the clang of the fire-wagon rang in Luke's ears as he pedaled up Burnside on his yellow bike. At Fred Meyer, the plank road turned to asphalt. But they were still coming.

At 23rd Street, a Chevy Nova pulled out and tried to block his escape. It was Slade, Garbage, and Monica, cruising NW Portland to find him.

Luke skidded around them and puffed up the hill. The Nova, burning oil, got passed by some Keystone cops on wooden bicycles.

The uphill chase now slowed to 4 miles-per-hour. Out in front, Luke made the turn for The Pittock Mansion. There a BATF agent waved him down with an M-16. "Restricted area!" the guy hollered. "Terrorist bomb site!"

"Listen," puffed Luke. "I just want to pick up my truck and my baby."

"A Riter Truck?" asked the fellow.

Luke nodded. The guy spoke into his walkie-talkie and waved him past.

His yellow truck wasn't in the dark parking lot. But the treetops on the other side of the mansion were lit up from below. Luke made his way around to the other side of the building.

Notified that a yellow truck containing a terrorist nitrogen fertilizer bomb was set to go off at the Pittock Mansion, the National Guard had deployed hours ago.

After the 1991 Gulf War in Kuwait, the Guard inherited a bunch of older M1 Abrams tanks and Hummers from the 3rd Armored Division. These days, the National Guard was rarely called up for active duty. The men polished their gear at monthly meetings and got to drive the tanks around during summer exercises. It was a novelty for these suburban guys to go into action.

To shield the residential neighborhood on the west side

of the mansion, they'd moved the truck to the other side of the structure. There they established their perimeter and set up lights.

The place looked like a Speilberg movie-set. Bright light-arrays glared down on the yellow vehicle. The National Guard aimed their M-16s with grenade launchers at it.

A weird guy in a trench coat and dark glasses pulled Luke aside. He was probably CIA. "You the one who drove the yellow Riter truck?"

Luke wasn't sure he should answer. Up on the roof of the Pittock Mansion, dark figures hovered. He hoped they wouldn't wreck the place. A loud engine roared.

My god, it was a Sherman tank! With a sweep of its turret it knocked down a 100 year-old Japanese Maple. The CIA guy checked something off on his clipboard, then spun around.

The Chevy Nova had pulled in, sputtering. Then Keystone cops, pedaling their antique bikes, arrived. Finally a clanging horse-drawn fire-wagon pulled up. "Whoa!" hollered the driver.

The CIA agent looked uncertain—pallid actually—as if he'd prefer that desk-job at headquarters in Langley. He finally spoke into his lapel, "Intruders have arrived, sir."

Slade and Garbage yelled out the Nova window. "We want our truck!"

"Where's that baby?" said Monica blankly, getting out. She looked about as if searching the soldiers for a familiar face.

As the tank pointed itself at Luke's truck, Professor Overton appeared under the bright lights. "Gentlemen," he told the soldiers. "You're surrounded!"

From the dark brush emerged a hundred ragged men swinging empty wine bottles.

"The Vanport Militia," announced Overton."

The National Guard immediately dropped their weapons. Luke hoped someone was making a movie of all this.

Garbage sized up the situation. "This calls for a genius," he said, shoving the CIA guy aside. "Unload that truck!" he hollered to government agents.

The federal explosive experts leapt to follow the orders of this bearded fellow in the Hell's Angels outfit. Garbage turned his attention to the standoff between the hobos and the National Guard.

Just then a crowd of 19th-century sailors, cowboys, and loggers arrived from Erikson's Saloon wheeling a keg of Weinhardt's beer. They were singing, "For You a Rose in Portland Grows!"

"Who likes beer?" yelled Garbage.

The National Guard and hobos surged forward.

Luke felt light-headed. At some ambiguous level—where things possessed less weight—he knew he'd failed again.

[continued on page 214]

[continued from p. 199.]

In the basement, Tech Support turned out to be the Wildman, I felt shock giving way to indignation. This was the guy whose capture in the woods was blocking me from seeing the news about my father.

So I pulled up a chair and faced the fellow—who, at least, was wearing a pair of shorts. "Are you The Guy in the Basement?" I demanded.

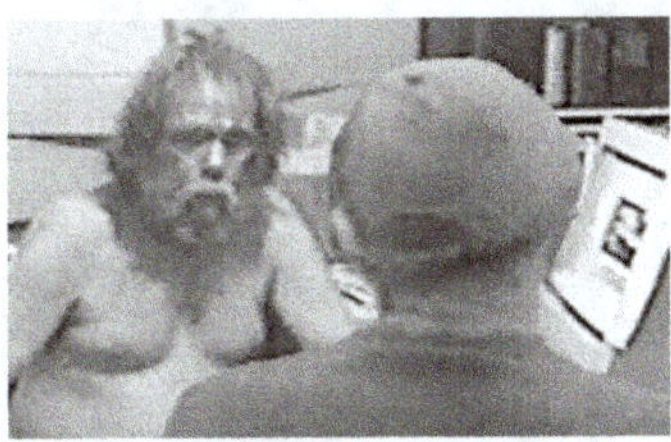

"Yup. I'm the one who sets up your magazine." He spoke in a silly gargle.

"One person doing everything?" I said. "That's all over. A relic of the 19th-century—Self Reliance, and all that. Any project now—magazines, movies, homework—they're all produced by teams."

His face went blank. "Team?" he said, feigning ignorance of the word.

In dismay, I realized he was just as deluded as Zapf, or Wynk. Those three ought to get together and trade hallucinations.

"Acknowledge Monkey-Mind," he said, "and it will blow away in the wind. *Just sit and listen to the birds.*"

I was touched because this fellow, without a trace of guile, was offering advice about the conduct of life.

But I sighed and said, "I beg you. You're a tech-guy, right? Please tell me how to scroll the browser."

"Oh those nasty shortcut-keys," he said. Then, fingers on the keyboard he demonstrated how to press **cntrl+tab +shift+del+shift+7.**

I rushed upstairs. The news was on the screen. Using fingers and nose, I pressed six keys at once.

though reports of damage
the school budgets are not
deal with catastrophic eve
Of course the possibility of
Evidently taxpayers will be

he's been observing the several years. "The time announce my find," . . .

Zapf has led a number of expeditions in search of the fabled Sasquatch of the NW. But this was the first time he revealed the extent of his contacts with the creature. We followed him through tangled brush, searching for our quarry. Finally the creature was spotted—just overhead. Abruptly it swung down from a branch, and there it was, the fabled Sasquatch of the NW. The thing was told to sit

during the interview that he howled at the moon crying the name, "Luna." The next morning he displayed his lap-top computer, then astounded us by his command of several skills, including playing the

Wheelchair Speedster Clocked Over the Limit

A North Dakota trucker claims he passed an elderly

This was maddening. But at least the headline about my dad was now in sight. I flexed my fingers and tried to think. Was it **tab+option+s**...?

Just then Zapf burst in the door. "Have I got news for you, buddy!" he hollered, waving a sheaf of papers.

"I'm busy," I said.

Behind him, the Guy from the Basement peeked in. "Oh boy. Take a look at these!" said Zapf. He slapped down three astro-logical charts.

"Now, they may look alike," he ex-plained. . "Three Aries: big-egos, en-ergetic, impatient, risk-takers. Two have Libra rising, ruled by Venus in the 5th or 6th house. That soft-ens the picture. The third one has Virgo rising ruled by Mercury. And it's conjunct the Moon! A Powerful intellect there—but cunning." Zapf went on and on about the charts.

I finally told him, "Zapf, I have no idea what you're talking about."

"What—you don't understand astrology? Why just picture yourself out in space, like the Fool on the Hill."

His description of the earth turning and the sun setting west of Manzanita in 1958 provoked a <u>vivid image in my mind</u>.

"April 18th?" said Zapf, making a peculiar face. "It's my birthday!," he cried. "That's all my foster parents knew." Sasquatch stepped in and Zapf threw an arm around the shaggy fellow. "So it's gotta be his birthday, too!"

"The Wild Man is *your brother*?"

"Oh," said Zapf. "We hit it off right away—years ago. We just knew."

"So you've come here to show me astrological charts?"

"These are Doc Stone's charts. I paid him a visit last night, and he finally fessed up. That file of his had more than one birth certificate. You remember what happened in 1958?"

"That Indian woman," I said. "She took off with some hoodlums."

"But first the grandmother disappeared," said Zapf. "She took one of the infant boys up the mountain,"

"I get it," said Monica. "She abandoned the baby, She knew the ancient prophecy, and she was old. So she never made it back down."

"Jeez," I said. "She left Sasquatch—to be raised by wolves."

"Beavers, mostly," said Zapf. "His chart says he was delivered at 4:15 p.m. Now the baby who popped out at 4:50—was me! They took me along."

"Oh yeah, I remember. They went north in a '49 Ford to Washington."

"And dropped me off," said Zapf. "In Goldendale. That's near Maryhill."

"Well," I said. "I'm happy you two found your birth records. Now if you'll excuse me, I've got to find out about my dad."

"I thought you'd want to know about him," said Zapf.

"You know about the wheelchair?"

"Nope. But I know about the third birth certificate."

"I don't have time for this. Would you and your brother just leave?"

Zapf didn't move. "You told me," he said, "that your own mother grew up in Tacoma. Obviously, that's where they dumped the third kid!"

"No mother would dump her kid."

"Well—" sighed Monica.

Zapf said, "She was drunk, fed up."

"Wait a minute. What third kid?"

"*You*, Strether. *Caxton is your dad.*"

"Oh no."

"Haven't you noticed how much we have in common? *Triplets* were born in Manzanita. <u>We're a family!</u>"

Zapf and his brother, Sasquatch, left before I could ask the backwoods computer genius about that keyboard code. After an hour I still couldn't crack it.

Monica and I looked for another TV. We went over and knocked on Sable's door. The house was locked up and dark. I'd given my dad a hundred-dollar bill. Was he staying in motels?

We headed back to Caxton's house. The added wings gave it the look of a villa. I tried to imagine growing up in a place like his—wide views of the city, lawns and shrubs that must have required a landscape architect.

"Good grief, me, one of Caxton's sons? Along with that naked weirdo. Three infants scattered across Oregon and Washington state. Is it possible?"

"Where's your birth certificate?"

"In a box somewhere. It says I was born in St. Paul—not Tacoma."

In my office, Monica put her arms around me. "This is fun isn't it?" she said. "Solving this puzzle together?"

"Hasn't Zapf already solved it?"

"Maybe not. But I was talking about *us*. We're solving it, right?"

I realized then that her presence made things dense again. How thin and unsubstantial I felt otherwise. Was I growing old and world-weary? Is that the way everyone felt these days?

The hours were going by. Days perhaps. Now it was dark outside. What had happened to my sense of time?

Again Zapf and his brother barged in.

"Woo-ee!" hollered Zapf. "Have we got news for the family!"

Quickly I called up the News-screen and gestured to Sasquatch. He came over and scrolled the browser for me.

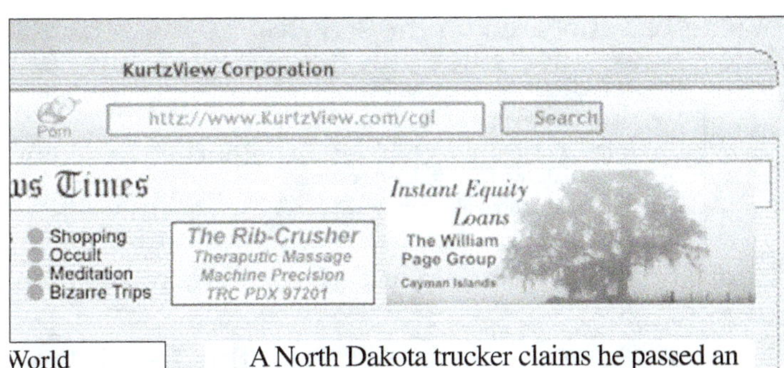

A North Dakota trucker claims he passed an elderly gentleman in a motorized wheelchair on Interstate 94 west of Bismark. He clocked the contraption at 57 miles per hour.

Now reports are coming in from other motorists. A housewife and her husband passed The Wheelchair

Speedster near the Montana border. They slowed down to catch this surprising and historic video footage. Click the picture.

And from Fargo comes this urban view of a fellow who makes his way through downtown streets in the dead of night. Apparently he slows down for stop signs.

Click the picture.

Check back for more developments in this epic saga of the open road.

A side-bar appeared on the screen:

> The big Freightliner and Peterbilt rigs have taken the old man under their wing. They shield him from the State Police, suggest secondary roads, and advise him about accommodations along the way.

"Hey," I said aloud. "That's encouraging, don't you think?"

Zapf and the Wildman glanced at the monitor, then at me. "But get this," said Zapf. "Sasquatch and I located the box this safety-deposit key fits."

He held up a key on a thong.

The Wildman snatched it.

Zapf explained that his brother had worn the key around his neck since birth—his grandmother's legacy to the infant she abandoned.

"Know what's in that box?" he said. "Why the original deerskin map of the Sasquatch kingdom! Now, the USA has a little problem. An Indian treaty they forgot to negotiate. It concerns a piece of Sasquatch real estate."

"Count me out," I said. "I've got genuine things to worry about here."

"Strether! You're a descendant! The three of us. We're the surviving members of the tribe!"

"Look at me, Zapf. Nobody is going to believe that I'm an Indian."

"That's right," he said. "Actually, you look a little Scandinavian. Like that red-headed Indian Lewis and

Clark encountered."

"Right," said Monica. "The Longfellow legend says they came from Iceland."

"But for the last few centuries," said Zapf, "all the other Native American tribes despised our ancestors. We drove stakes and claimed the land. Later they called us nasty, brutish, and hairy, scavenging in the woods."

Sasquatch stood scratching his ear. He was trying not to look offended.

"Okay," I sighed. "You and your new brother found an old map. What does it say you own? Smuggler's Cove?"

"More than that," said Zapf.

"Not the town of Manzanita?"

Zapf dug in his pockets. He yanked out a map of the Northwest. "Here," he said. "I've traced the boundaries with a pen knife. They seem to follow fault-lines beneath the earth.

"You're not serious," I said.

"Couple big earthquakes—this whole section of the USA could break off." He pulled at the section he'd traced with the knife. A large chunk of America <u>seemed</u> <u>to float</u> out to sea.

"And this piece of land—"

"About 40,00 square miles," said Zapf. That's what we own. The three of us. Of course, you gotta join the family."

"This is insane."

> Darker portents of the legend
> Told of quaking earth and ruptures
> Once the female line was ended.
> Then three brothers in contention
> Would devise a new beginning
> To an empire torn and fractured
> From the mainland. Like an island,
> Floating westward, rising, sinking,
> Land of Sasquatch, fate uncertain
> Would into the sunset wander …

"Strether, you don't remember the prophecy, do you?" Zapf said.

"And you're offering me this whole floating kingdom if I'll just admit that Caxton is my father?"

"Sure, Caxton's well-off. But this real estate comes from our Indian mom—they were never really married."

"Whatever happened to her?"

"Who knows? A drunk, a whore, dead in the gutter somewhere."

Wherever the words came from, I said, "Get thee behind me, Zapf."

Now Monica pointed to the computer. More news and <u>a video clip</u> appeared in the browser window.

As Zapf folded his map there was a distant sound.

"Listen," said Sasquatch.

"I don't hear nothing," said Zapf.

"Military trucks," I said. "To the east."

"It's the *Convergence*," whispered Sasquatch.

Zapf looked exasperated. "Aw Jeez! We saw the National Guard on our way up here. They were turning into the Pittock place. Didn't I tell you they were mixed up in this?"

"Mixed up in what?"

"It's the Corps of Engineers, actually. They moved a heap of Indian artifacts when they were building the Hanford Nuclear Site. Somebody must have tipped them off about the reappearance of the Sasquatch tribe."

"That sounds crazy," Monica said.

"Let's get down there," said Zapf.

Margo! the last episode

#20 Searching for Margo

[continued from p. 202]

Serial fiction by Anton Garamond

*THE FINAL EPISODE: The story so far: Luke has re-
turned to the Pittock Mansion, where Garbage has
taken charge of the BATF, FBI, National Guard, and
the Oregon Hobo Militia.*

Zapf and Strether drove down to the Pittock Mansion in
the orange Datsun. Sasquatch said he was taking a
shortcut—through yards and steep woods.

On the way, Strether felt dazed. He tried to remember how
he'd gotten involved with this character, Monica. Thank god,
he hadn't written her story. That would be a perverse twist.
But she'd said they'd discussed something "for months"?
Maybe her narrative ran in some alternate dimension?

The action seemed to be on the far side of the house.
They made their way around and confronted an unusual
scene. Under banks of bright lights, Hummers and an M-1
tank surrounded a yellow truck. But some sort of beer
party was going on.

"That looks like your truck," said Zapf.

Strether shook his head. "Not mine."

"Come on. You drove all your stuff out here in a yellow truck—the time you made the trip from Minnesota."

"What are you talking about?"

"Remember? You flew back to Minneapolis for

your father's funeral. It was last winter. You drove a yellow truck back."

Strether just shrugged. "What do you think is going on here?" he said.

Zapf strode over to the Mansion's veranda where a group of civilians stood. He asked an old guy in a white lab-coat what was going on.

"It's our college homecoming zelebration!"

Strether had to stare at a fellow about his own height coming up the steps in a black jacket like his own. But he looked beat, gravity sagging him—like maybe he hadn't slept in a couple days.

Luke trudged up the steps. His heart leapt as he approached Professor Overton and the bent old woman. She was still holding the baby. The professor didn't seem interested in whether or not Luke had delivered the Chinese coin.

Luke took the infant in his arms. It was scribbling on a piece of paper. "Hey, I'm writing all this down," it said. "Tell me what happened in episode number one, and I'll tell you who this woman is. Hint: she's Overton's daughter. Now, remember why you're here?"

Luke hugged the kid. "For you, I guess."

"Nah," said the baby. "The *ring*."

"Oh, sure," said Luke. He was tired.

Monica came over to announce that Overton had not only admitted her to the University, he'd named her Vanport's Homecoming Queen. "Hey Luke," she said. "About the baby. I just—like—found it. It's yours, if you want. Whatever."

"I guess," he said and watched Monica search the crowd for someone else—and walk off, From his finger, he now tugged off the old ring. "Ah, Olga," he sighed.

"Olga?" repeated the bent old hag.

"I was supposed to give this to someone named Margo." Luke had to think. Olga had called it a Hag's Ring.

"Well? Margo's right *here*," said the baby.

Now here came Margo Caxton up the steps with a grinning Wynk de Worde. She brushed past Luke and the bent old hag. Bill Caxton was tagging long.

"Zapf!" she cried, shaking a finger at him. You beat me to

Wynk's mother. Such a fascinating woman. Of course, we had to take Bill along."

Caxton looked dispirited. Then he brightened and put an arm around Wynk. both were wearing blue blazers. Father and Canadian gangster-imposter son.

"The three of us just drove back from Victoria," said Caxton. "We saw the lights over here and had to stop in."

"Now, about a husband's former lovers—" persisted Margo. "My advice is get them face to face. "They'll see right away the old spark is gone."

"That's the truth," said Caxton. "No offense to your mom, Wynk. But she's not exactly the Blond Indian Princess I remember from 1958."

Margo butted in. "She drew us a little map, Zapf. It shows the boundaries of her ancient tribe, the—"

"*Sasquatch*," said Zapf glumly. Damn, he thought. How had he missed realizing Mrs. Galton was a blond Scandinavian Indian? Wynk wasn't a con-man. He was the third triplet born near Neahkahnie Mountain. *Wynk was his brother.*

Caxton drew himself proudly up to his full height. "I was the bearded sailor who waded in through the surf at Smuggler's Cove. Can you imagine it? I re-enacted some sort of legend about Sir Francis Drake! And she had triplets!"

Zapf glanced at Strether. "Sorry," he said. "They didn't stop in Tacoma. They went to Victoria BC." He pulled out a birth certificate and star-chart. "Wynk, these belong to you. We better hug, *bro.*"

Strether wasn't paying attention. He couldn't take his eyes off the old hag facing this fellow who resembled him. *Luke*, Monica had called him.

The guy was gazing into the crone's eyes. "You?" he said, holding out the ring.

She accepted it. "This means *you're the one*," she croaked. "I'd given up on men. So Olga said she'd pick out a good one for me. I guess she picked you."

Luke took a breath. "There might be a problem. You're a bit older than I am."

"Oh, but I'm a *witch*," said the hag. "Whatever you want,

I can grant your fondest wish. All you have to do is kiss me. I might turn into a young woman."

"Do it," said the baby.

Zapf came over and joined Strether. "Is this guy gonna kiss the witch?" he asked.

Luke hesitated. The old hag's mouth was a mass of drool and winkles. She evidently had no teeth.

"Oh boy" said Zapf rubbing his hands. "This has gotta be the place where the <u>fireworks</u> begin."

A cry went up from the hobos and National Guard. The keg was empty. Arm in arm they headed down the hill. Garbage drove off in the truck. Where was Monica? wondered Strether. Luke's furniture and boxes sat stacked on the grass. The lights went off as federal agents packed up their gear.

"Hey," said Zapf. "Caxton understands about me and the Wildman being his sons, too. See, Culligan knew Wynk was Caxton's son right from the start—at Smuggler's Cove. But he wanted the biggest piece of the pie. So he just offered Wynk a flat fee to pose as somebody's heir. The idea appealed to Wynk—his mother had hinted odd things about his origins. It took him a while to realize that the part he was playing was his real life-story."

Luke was still frozen there, facing the bent old woman.

Zapf couldn't stand the suspense. "What the heck," he said. "I got a fondest wish, And I got a hankering for a kiss."

Zapf stepped smartly up to the hag, took her in his arms, and fervently pressed his mouth to hers. It went on for some time.

"You're a good kisser," she said. "But ain't you too old to believe in witches?"

"Aw," said Zapf, wiping his mouth.

"Besides," she said, her strange eyes on Luke. "This one is for me." She puckered her withered mouth at him.

Luke shot a glance at Strether, then, with a shudder, pecked her lips.

Then began a miraculous transformation. The bent old woman straightened and swept back luxurious hair. The lines on her face softened. Luke's knees felt weak—his fondest wish: a lovely forty-ish woman. He watched her luscious mouth form words: "I have a degree in Anthropology from the Sorbonne. And I like your baby."

Zapf had seen enough. He'd spotted Sasquatch and got him together with Wynk for the new family video. Caxton held back, declining to join them. "I just want to see <u>my three boys together,</u>" he said.

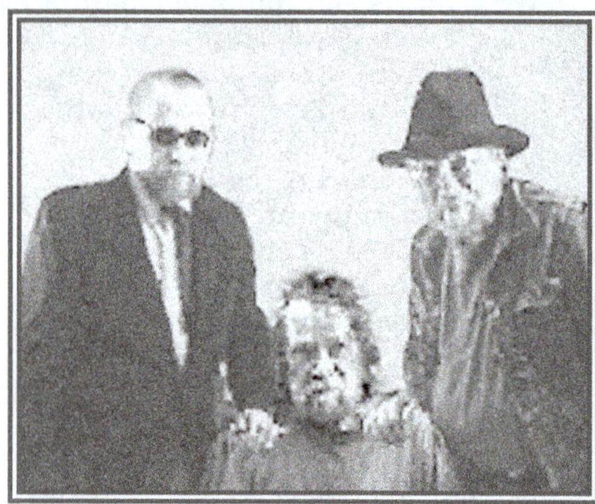

Meanwhile, Luke, the baby, and this 2nd Margo—formerly a hag—walked out to where they could see the lights of the city. It had been a long night.

"So, in a way," said Luke, "all this was a blind date?"

The new Margo gripped his arm. "It took Olga years to find the right man for me. Whom else could I trust? You probably even know what all women want. Am I right?"

Thinking of his own plight, Luke blurted out: "They want to get what they want."

"See?" she said. "You're *the one.*"

"And you're really Professor Overton's daughter?"

"I was named after my big fat grandmother," said Margo, "She was a powerful soul, and guarded the spirit of this place for 70 years—until I was born."

"But your father wants to prove he inherited this property, the entire city of Portland?"

"He dreams of tearing down the offices and condos, planting trees, and restoring the original Overton name: *Eden.*"

"And what does the spirit of this place tell you?" asked Luke.

"To be still," said Margo. "Just feel Her. The Mountain."

The sky was <u>brightening</u> in the east.

Luke was still and felt himself wanting to lean, the mass of Mt. Hood making him—for once—steady and sure, as if he wanted to be the reader to whom his book is true. ■

Strether's Ending

The next morning, things bustled again in the corridors of *The American Quarterly Review*. I ran into Gio Tag Liente and Erica Gill—the first old staff members to be hired back by Bill—with salary increases. They told me someone was waiting for a job interview in the conference room.

A minute later, I jolted to a stop in a doorway. *Monica.* She sat at the table, chin resting on fists she'd bundled into the sleeves of a striped top. Her half-amused smile, didn't match her emaciated appearance. Something had happened, overnight, to her body-builder's physique.

"Are you okay?" I said.

"I'm quite well, thank you," she said.

"And you're here for an interview?"

"Uncle Bill says you need an assistant."

"You're related to Caxton?"

"Sort of. An uncle three times removed—that sort of thing. I did work on the literary magazine at Amherst."

I was dumb-struck. My Monica, a college graduate?

"I just got my degree—class of 2002—honors in Philosophy".

"You actually wrote an honors thesis?"

"Yeah. *Bewitching Intelligence by Means of Language: Artifacts and Reality in Wittgenstein.*"

"Oh Jeez, you'll help me with topics like that?"

"I'd love to."

"You did say 'Class of 2002'? You'll have to pardon me, Monica. Ah, you're surprised I know your name. You see, I seem to have lost a year. "

"Oh dear."

"They tell me the magazine halted publication. Writers stopped writing. After— After that *event* in New York.

"You mean 9/11? I don't like to think about it either."

"I saw an old newspaper this morning. Horrifying."

"Maybe *that event* made you blank things out?"

"It's possible. I'd decided the blank was connected to my Dad dying."

"I'm sorry. It's hard to lose your father. Where you there with him?"

"That's the worst part. I wasn't there. Those damn nursing homes."

"Why don't you sit down."

I took a chair and faced her across the table. "You look different," I said.

She laughed. "How would you know?"

With a sigh, I realized then that I must have spent much of the last year hallucinating—or daydreaming. Still, I said, "Do I look familiar to you?"

"Funny you should say that."

"Because I do?"

"Everybody looks like someone else."

"In literature there are *double*s."

"Sure," she said. "And what about alternate universes? There could be hundreds of us—billions."

"I doubt Wittgenstein would approve of this conversation."

She laughed and rested her chin on her fists. "I like talking to you."

"Did you ever wonder," I said, "if people are like cartoons?

"There's a philosopher at Oxford," she said, "A guy who asks how we'd know if we're just a computer simulation. Well, I think I'm real."

"I wish you were," I said.

"Just click on <u>this word</u>—you'll see."

I glanced at her application form, . "It says here that you're—" I looked up again into her lovely eyes.

"—that I'm sexually active?"

"Oh, I wasn't going to ask that."

She shrugged, "I doubt we could work anything out. Do I get the job?"

The next day, I drove to the coast for a last look at the Pacific. If I waited until dark, I'd see that thin crescent moon—the old in the arms of a new generation. I wondered what that had to do with blanking out my dad's death. Surely the legacy of one generation to the next requires the heft of hard print.

I hadn't really known him. Oh, a few things—stories he told about growing up in Chicago, arguments over principle he had with my mom and people at work. But his generation didn't let out what they deeply felt.

Honor thy father and thy mother.
I've begun to realize this also applies after they're gone. How else justify hallucinating that crazy wheelchair odyssey for him? He always wanted to go out West. In a half-baked—perhaps desperate—way, I was trying to honor that old dream.

In another sense, his legacy to me wasn't any claim on property or cash in the bank. It was not letting other people define you. *Be who you are,* he'd said. An anxious way to live.

The tide's coming in now. The breeze is freshening, gulls hanging overhead. That bank of clouds offshore must be a front approaching. Gosh, I'll miss the sky out here.

Archived Document
[tedious footnote #9, p. 29]

Last week, when he'd visited the nursing home, there was trouble. Miss Spink, a tight little MSW wearing a red blazer, met Strether outside her office. "If he misbehaves again," she said, "we'll have to adjust his medication."

"Well," said Strether, as they walked to the elevator. "My father always was an active man. You know, working construction sites and so forth—"

"To begin with, I'll recommend a restraining device." Miss Spink's blazer sported epaulettes at the shoulder. She marched ahead like a cadet, her hair shaped with gel into a kind of helmet.

"What sort of device?" he asked, falling as much as possible into step.

"It's just a belt. A seat-belt for wheelchairs. He's been getting up, you know. Trying to walk."

"That's good, isn't it? After the stroke?"

"It's very disruptive. On Monday, he got into a vacant wheelchair outside the dining room. A motorized chair. It belonged to a resident who— Who isn't with us any longer."

"You mean my dad drove off in the thing?"

"Around and around, on the main floor. At a frightening speed. It took three orderlies to stop him."

"Really."

"And the next day we found him fiddling with it again, pulling on some belt attached to the motor."

"Maybe it needs an adjustment. He was an engineer. Just give him some tools or—"

"Now about his unpaid bill."

Strether rubbed his brow. "I thought that was settled. He's *spent down*." The phrase meant that his father's only bank account—Strether's inheritance—was exhausted. At this point of utter destitution, the state was supposed to step in and make the payments. If Strether's mother were alive, they'd drain off her money first. Some aging couples delayed this process by splitting their assets and getting divorced. It was a crazy way to grow old together.

The elevator was blocked by a chrome traffic jam of wheelchairs and old ladies gripping walkers. Miss Spink stepped past them and put a key in a lock to call the elevator. Strether wondered how long this throng of people had been waiting there, staring at an elevator button that wasn't even functioning.

From the other corridor, a gorgeous woman appeared, pushing her mother in a wheelchair. The young woman's thick auburn hair was pulled back with cloisonne combs, and she wore soft fabrics of beige and salmon. Maybe she was a New Yorker. Emeralds flashed at her ears. Her complexion glowed like a sunset, and she'd made up her lips a bright shade of persimmon. Before her sat a frail little creature, entirely bald, toothless, her mottled skin bleached a deathly white. Strether wrenched his gaze from one to the other, as if plunging from the surface of things to their inner core. He thought of Melville's whiteness, of nature painting like a harlot to mask the charnel-house—the skinhead alien—within. Wonder then at his agonized flight into a stairwell to reach the second floor?

Upstairs, Miss Spink stepped out of the elevator. She'd come up alone, like it was her private car. "Now about your father's episodes—" she said, falling into step beside Strether. In every room they passed, there were two beds—each with a pair of outstretched legs—and two dressers against the wall with a TV on top. The TVs were on.

"He didn't hit someone again, did he?" asked Strether.

Last week Strether's father had punched his roommate when the guy wheeled ahead in line outside the dining room. He'd whirled the fellow's chair around and threw a right cross that struck above the ear and sent the guy crashing against the wall. Fortunately the roommate suffered from a bone condition that made him rubbery—he could fall down a flight of stairs and laugh it off. But Strether always put on a face of surprised indignation when told about his dad's violent spells.

Of course, his father's public displays of aggression went way back. When he was a kid, Strether would sit in the car, terrified, when his father leapt out at a red light to try provoking a fist-fight with a motorist who'd passed him on the right. The man grew up in South Chicago before World War I. The men worked in the steel mills and came home drunk. The Swedish kids fought with the Catholic Polacks. You learned how to rough people up, how to physically restrain your own father. As a boy, Strether had seen his dad shove his mother around when they argued, but he never hit her with his fist. Mostly his dad busted things up—dishes, furniture—then left the house to cool off. Young Strether assumed that his parents were the only ones who fought like this. It was a great source of shame. And the house—his mom on the phone, wheeling and dealingc—was a mess. He never allowed his friends inside.

Miss Spink paused at a doorway. "Your father hasn't threatened anyone lately," she said. "But we're concerned about his physical strength. He's been bending silverware in the dining room."

At the age of 94, Strether's father seemed to think he was still an athlete, a gymnast. Painful arthritis in his knees discouraged him from walking. But he faithfully did isometric exercises (for pecs, abs, triceps, biceps) in his wheel-chair, keeping his upper body in terrific shape.

"Bending silverware?" said Strether. "He's just showing off. "You ought to get him on some parallel bars."

"This is not an athletic club," declared Miss Spink.

"Maybe it should be. Look, I know you've got a fine staff: social workers, speech pathologists, therapeutic recreation-ists. You've got group singing, arts and crafts, church serv-ices. But that's the problem. This place is set up like a church social. Why not a shop with power tools? Or a room with leather chairs where men smoke cigars and shoot pool? Or a place set up like barber shop where then guys sit around and tell fishing stories?"

"Most of our residents, Mr. Strether, are not men."

It was true. Most men didn't make it this far. They were, it turned out, the frailer, weaker sex. Maybe if a guy had been a Don Juan, then a place like this, women everywhere you looked, would be heaven.

Actually, his dad was a dapper fellow before he got mar-ried late. And apparently musical. In the 1930s, he wrote songs and sent them off to publishers. "They stole my stuff," he told his son. "You know that one that goes 'So deep is the ocean? How high is the sky?' I wrote that."

"Dad, that's Irving Berlin."

"Here's another one:

> With every Christmas card I write,
> I'm dreaming of a winter way out west.
> Where the grass is still green,
> and the snow is never seen . . .

and so forth."

What could you say to that? Did they have a piano in this nursing home? His dad could pick out melodies with one finger.

"Okay," Strether finally told Miss Spink. "Please, can't you just give him a bed by a window."

"He's on the list. For an opening." This meant they were waiting for some other guy to die. But having a private view out a window was the one thing in this place that might have given Strether's father some joy. He loved to watch the sky, thunderheads building up for summer storms. He studied the weather map in the newspaper and could indicate, in a bank of clouds to the west, a passing cold front. In his retirement condo, he had an open view to the west from the 5th floor. When a storm approached, he'd turn off the lights and pull a chair up to the big window. "The eye is the first circle," he said. "The horizon the second." He'd read some Emerson.

Strether was staring at the epaulettes on Miss Spink's cadet outfit. "Is that your only way to solve problems around here, waiting lists?"

She made a little stamp with her foot. "Hey, do you think this is an easy job?" she said. "You get fond of these people and then watch them wither away? Well just try it." She did an about-face and marched off the way they'd come.

Strether watched her leave, trying to figure out if she'd finally opened up and confessed her secret: that the hard shell she wore like armor was actually a way of holding herself together.

Inside the room, his father sat hunched in his wheelchair beside his bed. There was no sign of the rubber roommate. He controlled access to the window. "Hey, how you doing?" said Strether, pulling up a chair.

The old guy—face blank, a little grim—stared at his intellectual, skinny son as if he regretted not teaching the boy how to throw a punch.

"I've been talking with that woman, the administrator,

about getting you a better room—with a window. She says you're on a waiting list."

His father said, "Buh-buh-buh." He possessed only this ambiguous phrase and the word, "Nah," to communicate all his needs. Deep in the folds of his left brain, the language centers—deadened when a clump of hemoglobin congealed at a branching artery—had shut down. Strether pictured the cerebral tissue as a blackened landscape, buildings in rubble like the burnt libraries at Alexandria, maybe something on the scale of a city and its infrastructure all bombed out, nuked to twisted girders. Elsewhere, far from the blast-zone, a few primitive sites were trying to reassemble the old skills, Neanderthal scholars crouched in the dirt working ciphers fashioned from twigs ("Buh") and stones ("Nah").

"I came to tell you that I have to leave town," said Strether. He was staring at the floor, hands clenched. "I'll have to drive all weekend to reach the west coast by Monday." Strether looked up for the reaction.

His father's face was blank, something gone in the eyes. He'd always talked of going out west—to California or Oregon. Could he move his dad out there?

"I can fly back at Thanksgiving," said Strether. "At Christmas for sure." There was no reply. "Maybe there's something you need?"

The old guy stirred in his chair. He hated to ask for favors.

"So, you do need something. Tell me, is it animal?"

"Nah."

"Vegetable?"

"Buh-buh."

"Okay. Socks, maybe? "

"Nah," said his father, looking alert.

They often played twenty-questions like this to get at a

single word. After ten minutes Strether understood that his father needed something smaller than a bread box that was not related to personal hygiene or to clothing. Yet everybody had it. Paper was a possibility—some kind of legal document? Strether looked about the room, its two beds, two dressers jumbled with memorabilia, two easy chairs. When you move a parent into a place like this, they hand the family a list of permissible items: Last Things. It was like furnishing a tomb. Then it came to him. You put a coin in the mouth of the dead to pay for passage over the river in the lower world.

"Money," Strether said aloud. Everybody had some.

"Buh-buh-buh!"

Strether got out a five-dollar bill. His father snatched it. With his big hands he smoothed the bill flat on his thigh, then held it up to the light. On the back-side, Strether could make out the lacy borders woven like intricate wicker, where conch-shells sprouted plaster leaf-shapes framing a vista of the Lincoln Memorial. For an instant, in this cell-like room, he felt certain that one might actually enter that certain slant of light—oh, on a day in early February, about an hour or so before  noon—that you might climb the marble steps while sun shot from low over the Potomac, such a sweetness in the air as you pass between plinth and column to face...

"Buh." His father, in his chair, thrust out an open palm like a panhandler.

"More?" said Strether. He again looked in his wallet. What

the hell, he thought, taking out one of his hundred-dollar bills.

His dad let out a long sigh as he accepted it. His eyes looked a little glassy. In his prime during the Depression, maybe he'd never held a hundred-dollar bill in his hands. To him it probably felt like a thousand dollars.

"Now keep that in a safe place," warned Strether, certain some orderly would pocket it by nightfall.

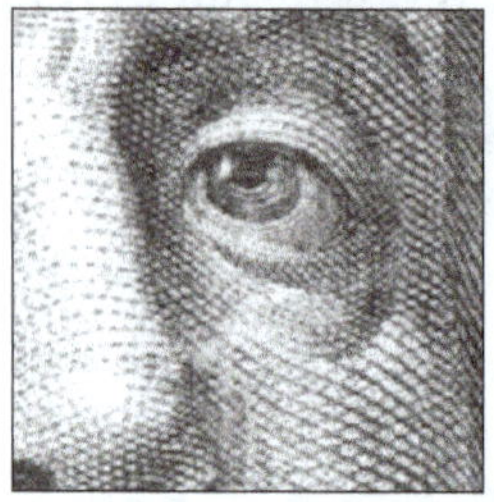

His father folded the bill and stuffed it deep into his pants. He flashed a rare smile, as if amused by the thought of Benjamin Franklin's left fish-eye now pressed against his 94-year old thigh. Then he gestured his son out of the room.

"But—"Strether said. He'd planned to ask the important questions: Had he been a good son? Had his father made peace with the world?

The old guy was holding his hand aloft in farewell.

"You're right," said Strether, getting up. "I have to go. I'll call you next week. Yes, I'll drive carefully. You take care, now."

"Buh-buh-buh." His father's last words. *Be who you are,* he'd once told Strether. Is that what he was trying to say?

Outside, Strether spotted Miss Spink getting into an expensive little red Mercedes convertible. Either he'd underestimated the woman's salary or people were slipping her gifts under the table in exchange for little favors. Dumb, he told himself, thinking of "Bartleby." You're supposed to bribe the jailer. So that's what it took—a new car for a bed by the window? He and his father were out of their league.

Just now in the parking lot there was that certain slant

of light. Strether felt its heft from overhead. Through the trees came the muffled roar of the expressway. Then there was a lull. The sound went flat—like the landscape in Minnesota where time passes slowly. Beyond these malls and asphalt the distance went west—on and on. ■

Quiz #1

1. Who reported seeing the mummified
   testicles in Rapallo?

   a.   Caxton

   b.   Strether

   c.   Pound

   d.   Auden

> Read ahead. The correct answer to this question is on page 17.

2. Maddi Goedjeff's office is

   a.   downtown.

   b.   the last on the right

   c.   empty

   d.   windowless

> You will find the correct answer only on the digital version—page 15.

3. When Margo says J7ɔıꞧ

> To decipher this, consider the context.

   a.   Strether laughs

   b.   Strether is perplexed

   c.   She's quoting G. B. Shaw

   d.   a warning appears.

> You will find the correct answer to this question on page 14.

(You probably turned to this page from "...a woman screamed." p. 16.)

Answers   1. c. 2. b. 3. d.

(Before reading Longfellow you'd better take the Pop Quiz)

Hey, let's review the International Phonetic Alphabet!

Wynk   thinks   Bill   is   his   father

wɪŋk θɪŋks bɪl ɪz hɪz faðɚ

Can you handle these alternate phonetic symbols?

Here's the quiz:

1.   The best English spelling of this sound is

   a. flicker
   b. floozy
   c. blinker

2.   The best English spelling of this sound is

   a. bird in hand
   b. jim-a-jam
   c. fuck-a-duck

(You probably came to this page from "Longfellow's Sasquatch" on p. 84.)

Answers:

1. c 2. c.

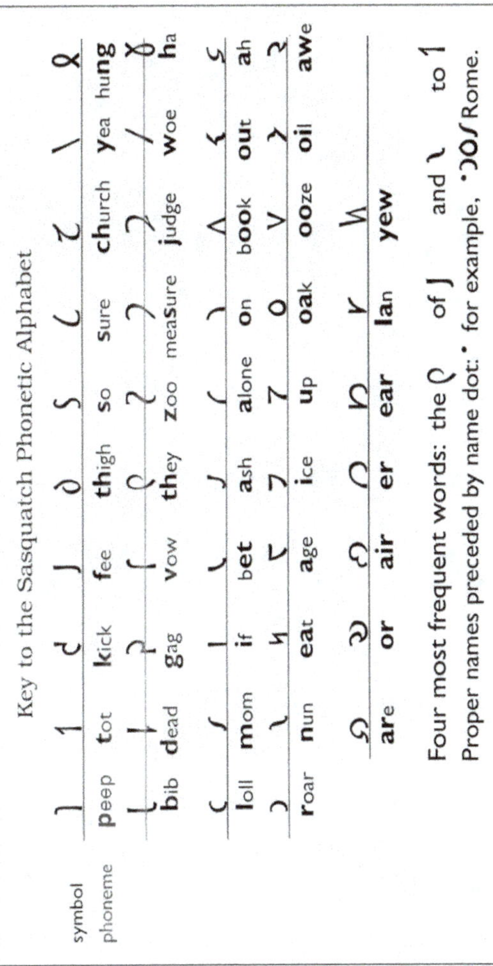

Key to the Sasquatch Phonetic Alphabet

The Sasquatch Alphabet and typeface was adapted by the author from the Shaw Alphabet as published in Bernard Shaw's *Androcles and the Lion*, The Shaw Alphabet Edition, (Penguin Books Ltd: Harmonsworth, Middlesex, 1962)—which encouraged other works to be transliterated into the Shaw Alphabet without permission.

Barrett, Magrath, Pugmire, and Read were the winners of a 1958 competition, set out in Shaw's will, to design a more efficient alphabet for English. (Kingsley Read's design dominated the final form.) Here, standard midwestern American English had been substituted for the pronunciation Shaw preferred: Northern English as spoken by "His Majesty our late King George V."